# Luna Station Quarterly

## Issue 025 | March 2016

### Editor & Publisher

Jennifer Lyn Parsons

### Assistant Editors

Tara Calaby
Cathrin Hagey
Andi Marquette
Dana Mele
Megan Patton
Danielle Perry
Iona Sharma

### Cover Artist

Sara Kipin

LUNA STATION PRESS

Luna Station Quarterly publishes short fiction on March 1st, June 1st,
September 1st, and December 1st. For more information and submission
guidelines, please visit our website at lunastationquarterly.com

For Luna Station Press

Creative Director - Tara Quinn Lindsey

 LUNA STATION PRESS

576 Valley Road #197

Wayne, NJ 07470

www.lunastationpress.com

info@lunastationpress.com

# CONTENTS

# EDITORIAL

Jennifer Lyn Parsons

LSQ has always been an inclusive community with one small (or not so small) caveat. You must be female to have your work published with us. As time has gone on, we have had internal discussions about making statements on what that means exactly.

In the end, the call was made to keep the language throughout our site and publications on the female end of the spectrum. We have indeed published a few authors who skirted the edge of more conservative definitions of womanhood and, if the story is right, we'll do that again.

I'm sure there are a lot of people out there that would prefer we make a clear stance on if we'll accept stories by authors who are transgender or gender fluid. My answer to that is actually pretty simple. "Do you feel like you identify with what it means to be a woman, by your personal definition?" and "Do you feel comfortable in the community we've created here?" If the answer to those questions is yes, then please send us your story or sign up to write for the blog.

The mission of LSQ is to support female genre fiction writers and their stories. It is this editor's belief that being female has little to nothing to do with what your body looks like. There are a lot of hard-to-define factors that go into anyone's personal definition of if they are female or not, and many of those are driven by complex feelings often mired in the constraints of our culture's definitions of gender.

In the last six years of publishing LSQ, I have had a front-row seat to the amazing strides women are making to gain personal freedom and safety. It's an honor to watch as women ask the hard questions, not only of the men around them, but also of their governments, society at large, other women, and especially themselves.

And some women are coming up with answers that are hard to process, and realizing that defining themselves as a 'woman' suddenly doesn't fit the way it used to, though nothing else really feels right either.

That leaves me with a question to ask myself in regards to what "woman spaces" mean and if they still work. In short, yes, they do still work and they're still needed. Women-oriented places like LSQ are still important. There is still work to be done, there is still inequality all around us, and there is still a need for women's voices to have a place held for them.

It just may mean that the woman who wrote one of the stories you are about to read may or may not fit so squarely into that round hole of "woman" as you might assume. And we welcome her and the story she has to tell.

LSQ|025

# MAMA CUCA

## H. Pueyo

Argentine-Brazilian writer,
translator, and multiculturalism
enthusiast. Her work as a comic
scriptwriter was published
in Portuguese by Editora
Draco, and in English by the
successfully crowdfunded
Dates Anthology.

The wall reads:

MAMA CUCA
CARD & COWRIE-SHELL READINGS
BRINGS BACK LOVED ONE IN 03 DAYS
DOES ALL KINDS OF WORK, NO
MATTER HOW HARD
SATISFACTION 100% GUARANTEED
TEL. 33XX-09XX
YOU DON'T NEED TO SAY A WORD, SHE WILL
TELL YOU EVERYTHING!

All written in impact-like font, capital letters, her name in cerulean, the text in black, the number in red, and the shadows in bright, mustard yellow. This kind of announcement is common in the entire town as marketing for all sorts of services and stores, mostly in posters glued to posts or painted on walls, so the gaudiness of it can be easily overlooked. At distance, actually, the house looks pretty bland: underneath the rough white paint, the wall is made of bricks and cement, and the lower part is stained by moss and dirt. Treetops appear from behind, and a small door is seen in the middle.

Trembling, Maju looks around. She's heard of Cuca before, she's even holding a ripped poster with the same sayings as the painting, only printed in cheap monochrome instead.

She's never come this far before, though, always out of fear. "No one messes with Cuca," she overheard a kid saying at school, during lunch break. "Even politicians fear her. She can do anything. Also," he added, talking and chewing, "some people say she has an alligator head".

And there she is, twelve years old in a month and a half, green bicycle in one hand, and the pamphlet in the other. It took a forty-minute ride on a massive dirt road with a few dry trees around, only to find a vast property outside of their little town. *Spooky.* Maju folds the piece of paper and puts it back in the pocket of her white t-shirt.

All of that to prove to some superstitious classmates that a fortuneteller has a normal human body. *Alright.* She might as well do the entire job, then.

Maju walks to the grated front gate, looks at the small camera, and rings the bell.

– Mama Cuca, readings and services?—It's a masculine voice, and she wants to run back home, before considering it might be the secretary.

– Ah… Um, I called yesterday,—she stutters, painfully aware of how childish her voice is sounding. Her sneakers are white and pink, to fit the rest of her garment: a cotton t-shirt with two small pockets over her hip bones, a white hippie skirt covering her bony knees, and a school backpack. Under the skirt, she's also wearing pink shorts, but they hardly show.—I have an appointment for Maria Júlia.

– Card reading for Maria Júlia. I'm opening the gate.

Cuca is a weird name for a fortuneteller. Anyone in Brazil has already heard that noun, either because of the coffee cake, or the folkloric monster. An old witch with an alligator body and the most terrifying mood, willing to take badly behaved children away from their parents. Maju opens the door after hearing the click. Her dad used to sing her a lullaby about the creature, something along these lines: *sleep, baby / or the Cuca will get you / Daddy went to the field / and Mommy's off to work.*

Chuckling, the girl is already inside, front gate locked. The house has only one floor, and is prettier than its outside, with creamy walls and a roof made of bricks. Not the most welcoming place, for sure, but better. It's surrounded by low grass, with palm, guava and lime trees. Maju parks her bicycle against a trunk, and runs to the man waiting outside.

– Um, hi.—Maju attempts a polite smile, showing parts of her tiny teeth. She's not particularly tall for her age, but the man is almost her size, with the exception of width. He's brawny, with broad shoulders, slim waist and thick arms, very muscular and tanned, looking orange-brown.

– Mama Cuca is waiting for you,—he says, looking like someone who takes his job very seriously for a bald, shirtless man who answers the telephone for a Tarot reader. Maju's palms are sweating when he points to the open door.—You first, miss.

– Well, um, sure.—Maju holds her backpack fiercely. The man has been nothing but courteous , but the situation frightens her, as it goes against every single motherly rule of not talking to strange men nor going too far away alone.— And you are?

– Ricardo. *Assistant,*—he adds, as if trying to prove some-thing. His eyebrows are very bushy and black, and curl when he says the word. Inside, the living room has two sofas covered with textured sheets for clients to wait comfortably. Ricardo has a desk of his own, with two telephones, a com-puter, a printer, and even a smartphone. He sits on the office chair, and begins to type.—You're pretty young to be here, aren't you?

– I'm not.—Her words are quick, although he isn't aggressive at all. Rather, he sounds sympathetic. It's still very weird to talk to someone barely dressed.—I mean, I am, but I'm not. Too young, I mean, just… young.

– No judgment.—Ricardo's baldness shines a little bit under the warm reflection of the sun entering through the window. The entire house smells like incense.—If you're here, it must be something important. Cuca is very picky with her clients.

*Not really.* The thought crosses Maju's mind, as a euphoric reassurance of her skepticism. She is convinced that stories of monsters and inhuman powers are child's play—*and twelve is hardly a child, right?*—even when a small tickling of nervousness is rolling down her neck. That's what Mom says, at least. At twelve, you need some maturity, and she is putting that knowledge into practice.

Besides, discovering something huge like magic (or lack of it) will surely put her in the spotlight, at least in class. Making friends is hard when everyone already has a clique, and all the boys and girls have been obsessed with meeting Cuca, without any success.

– What kind of person is Mama Cuca?—The question causes Ricardo to chuckle and rest his large hands over the purple velvet covering the table.

Next to his computer, there are small statues of saints: the dark Our Lady of Aparecida with her crown and blue cloak, a scarlet devil-like man with a hat, and a laughing woman wearing only a small piece of red loincloth. The last two are Exu and Pomba Gira, very similar to the statues her mother also has at home. Maju is used to the imagery, because the building they own is divided in three different floors. Upstairs, where the family lives. The main store, focused on selling religious artifacts for Umbanda and Candomblé, like candles for rituals, herbal baths, statuettes, and musical instruments. And, finally, downstairs in the basement, the temple they use at night and during the weekends.

Maju was raised there; her mother has been the *mãe-de-santo*, the main priestess, since before Maju was born, and puts in a lot of effort to keep the belief alive in their town. The temple is always full, and Maju is eager to help in her free time, impressed by the chanting, the dancing, and the usual ceremonies for different entities. They never allow her to participate in the Exu and Pomba Gira rituals, though, claiming that she is still too young for that.

– Oh, you'll see.

– And, um, I… Do I need to pay now?

– Don't worry about that.—Ricardo is playing with the smartphone now. Maju stops squeezing the panda-shaped purse inside her backpack.—It's like Cuca always says. "The client will know the price after the results."

– But it's not too expensive, right? I don't…

She is going to say more and explain details of her monthly allowance, but a deep, disembodied voice interrupts her:

– Maria Júlia? *Mmmmariiiiaaa Jjúúúúliiiaaa*, I'm waiting for you…

Ricardo makes a sign for her to go, pointing to an entrance with a thin curtain as a door. Maju waves yes, getting up. Before entering, she breathes in, and fixes her hair. Her light brown afro was combed into a high and puffy ponytail by her mother earlier in the day, making some tight ringlets pop over the top of her head. The rest of the hair, the part that had been pulled back so much it hurt, is braided. The man seems to notice she's nervous, and he smiles reassuringly in a way that reminds her of her dad. *Alright*, she thinks, slapping her own round cheek, a couple of tones darker than her eyes and curls, *here I come*.

– I'm going!—she shrieks, noticing now how scared she truly is. "My aunt says she sold her soul to the Devil," Maju remembers her classmate saying, making gestures with the hands to imitate horns. "That's why she has powers now. Powers… And *that* head."

The sneakers make a plastic sound, and the lace of her skirt brushes against the Bermuda shorts underneath. Maju trembles, but she swallows her fear, and walks through the curtain.

A wave of smoke hits her in the face, a mixture of garlic, rue, gully root, rosemary, and a little bit of common cigarette. Quickly, in the fog, she realizes it's coming from a silver object hanging from the ceiling. She still can't see Mama Cuca, only a shadow behind the white and gray remainders of incense. Maju feels the synthetic rug under her shoes, and uses one of her hands—the one that's not holding the strap of her backpack—to flap the air, trying to breathe.

– Maria Júlia…—The penetrating voice of Mama Cuca fills the entire environment, making it seem smaller, caging her with smoke, furniture and walls.—Maria Júlia Salles… Your mother and your father call you Maju, little Maju, don't they? Can I call you that, too?

Maju freezes. Her knees don't respond to her brain's pleas for action, and her lungs burn from the incense. *I'm used to this*, she thinks, narrowing her close-set eyes, trying to ignore what seems to be a crocodile-like form on the other side. *We always have incense at home.* Suddenly, the smoke is not as thick anymore, and she starts to see the room.

– Um, yes… I mean, of course!—Maju walks forward, seeing a flashy armchair in front of a round table. All the windows are covered by dense drapes, and candles are the only things illuminating her room.—Hi.

And there is Cuca. No giant alligator head, no sign of demonic activities, no supernatural element to it. Just a woman—but a very big one, indeed. Mama Cuca, as she sees, is sitting behind the table and surrounded by images of the most different entities: Catholic saints, a very cheap Buddha statuette, two white maneki-nekos, and an impressive collection of different Exu and Pomba Gira made out of painted plaster. The whole setting makes her look somewhat unreliable and fake. There are lit incenses and candles of all colors on the floor, close to the straw armchair she's sitting on.

As for her, she is large in every sense. Her limbs are plump, her fingers are stubby, her neck is wide and short with a fold in the middle, her chest is hefty, her belly broad and inflated, without a single flap appearing under the shoulderless top. Instead, her whole body looks hard and strong, like she could choke a bull with her bare hands. More than that, Mama Cuca is tall, adding to the perception of her bigness, even when sitting down. Her hair, dyed a very yellow blonde, looks like cooked noodles falling over her shoulders, covered partially by a pink turban with an artificial flower in the front. Her exposed orange-white skin is marked by considerable decades and freckled by the sun, but it's hard to define her correct age.

– Sit down, doll,—she purrs, pointing to the other chair with her absurdly long and pointy nails. Her toes are also claw-like, and equally painted with rose polish and rhinestones. Maju has been avoiding eye contact so far, but when she looks up, she finally sees more of Cuca's face. Her eyes are piercing and amber, with blue eyeliner adorning the lower eyelid. The eyebrows are nonexistent, and have been replaced by brown, arched tattoos. Cuca is not pretty, but she is, most definitely, terrifying, alligator head or not.

– Um, sure.—The little girl obeys. Her head is hurting from the tight ponytail, but the pain makes her feel safer.

– Want a coffee, darling? Cappuccino? A soda, maybe? Oh, I bet you like guarana better than coke, don't you?—She does, it's true; she's never liked cola as much as she likes the national soft drink. Maju waves her head, and the hair moves with her.— Jorge… Jorge!

Another man appears, dressed in a similar fashion to Ricardo. Unlike the secretary, he is neither short nor bald, and has dark finger coils falling over his forehead. But, like Ricardo, he only wears trousers, and his skin is shiny from being outside.

– Bring our little friend a can of guarana, yes, dear? Oh, and tell Ricardo to open the front door. The afternoon breeze is bliss.

While Cuca talks, Maju pays attention to small details: the tie-dye pattern of her top, the silicon straps of her bra sinking into her skin, the tacky butterfly tattoo on the back of her leg, the feet-long skirt draped in a way that shows up to her knee. When Jorge is gone, she looks back to Maju.

– Maju, why are you here?—It's funny how something said in such a soft voice can sound so threatening. The tiny curls of her nape rise in a shiver. Cuca picks up a box of cigars, and puts one in the middle of her yellowed teeth. If she could get closer, she would smell the specific scent of tobacco, similar to the ones used in rituals.—What goes through that little head of yours?

Mama Cuca is looking at her, no, *into* her; she's opening a hole through her mild brown eyes. In return, Maju smiles. The woman uncovers the table, throwing the cloth over the arm of her own chair, and brushing the statues aside. Underneath, there is a carved wood plate with white and brown cowrie-shells, and a battered Tarot deck. The way she keeps everything seems to be skipping all the rules Maju knows of divination, but Cuca doesn't care.

– Ah, I'm here for… a reading?—Her voice is unsure, and her short nails, the result of prolonged nail-biting, scratch the fabric of her skirt, pulling it up accidentally and showing the lower part of the long pink shorts, along with her scrawny knees.—Just, like, um… in general?

– I see. A reading it is, then.—One of Cuca's hand covers the cowries, and then throws them on the table with no kind of preparation. The other touches the deck. *This is all wrong,* Maju thinks, with rules yelling behind her eyes. *What is she doing?* What is she, really, because even the Tarot makes no sense. She is mixing cowries and cards, she's not shuffling the latter, she's just casting them together.—Maria Júlia Salles da Cunha, only daughter of Regina Salles Rossa and Antenor Soares da Cunha. Born September 2nd… A Virgo, I like that…

Maju's untouched eyebrows curl, almost creating a single line with the help of the hair that has been growing between them in the last year.

– How do you know all of that?

Cuca chortles.

– I know your parents, doll. Good ol' Regina is weary of the likes of me, has been tellin' the whole town to keep away from my house. Ever since that occasion, years ago…—Another deep, husky laugh. Maju wants to know more, wants to ask how they met, but she's unsure if that counts as part of the appointment.—And Antenor, darling man… Oh, Jorge, you took too long! Poor little Maju would die of thirst, if it was for you! Did Ricardo distract you again with those silly videos? He's obsessed with the cat ones, I'm telling you.

Maju didn't see Jorge entering the room through the smoke. He smiles at Cuca's comment, putting a glass of guarana with plastic ice cubes in front of her. They are shaped after fruits, of two different colors. She thanks him, but he is already gone.

– You were telling me about Dad…

– Oh, yes, Daddy has to keep his two eyes open. Tell him to

drop the salt, maybe start a diet. Actually…—She raises one hand to the air, and Maju swears she is seeing the incense burn a gray figure that looks like her father, choking, his hand grasping his own chest. Then, it's gone.—A cardiologist would be the wisest choice, I'd say. Or in two years, your Father's Day might be a tad lonely, know what I mean?

Horrified, Maju bobs her head. Not that she believes in it too much, but there is something about Cuca that is starting to feel painfully real.

– Old Regina is not leaving you alone lately, is she?—Cuca continues, and the guarana pops bubbles against the glass and the plastic grapes. The turban she wears is really badly done, Maju considers. It looks as if she pulled it back, and now it covers only a small part of her head.—The only peace you get at home is when you're out, because Mommy is always complaining about everything you do. You need to study, you need to do the dishes, you need to act your age… Always so picky, ain't she?

– Ye-yes…—she agrees. The last year and a half have been unbearable, in many aspects, to the point where the only time she's not fighting with Mom is during holidays, celebrations and at the temple. Then, they can have fun like before, but in daily life, she seems to have switched from mother-of-a-child to mother-of-a-teenager pretty quickly.—How…?

– Cuca sees everything, darling doll.—She points her fingers to her forehead, scratching her skin with her long nails.—Nothing hides from Cuca. And, you're angry, aren't you? Normal for your age, and worse! You feel lonely. Not talking to anyone at school, only listening. Hard to make friends, is it?

– Very hard.—Maju looks down. She has to wake up six in the morning every day to get ready for school, and all her being yells against it. No one mistreats her there, but they don't talk to her either, and she feels invisible, like furniture, like part of the cracked walls.—I don't know why. Maybe I'm just not interesting enough?

– Ah, worry not.—Cuca blows out one of the candles, and the room gets darker. Maju can see the shape of her own head on the wall: the round forehead, the full ponytail.—This *will* change. Not if Daddy gets sick, though; if our friend Antenor mishandles his health, you will only grow angrier, and lonelier. Your upsetting mother will be even pickier, even more impatient. Ah, child, this won't work out, no. You all need harmony.

– But how? How is it going to change? I don't think I can do anything.—Maju's body feels weak, but the sugar in the carbonated drink helps her go back to normal.—Mama, I don't know what to do.

– Oh, but that's why you're here, isn't it, Maju?—Her voice seems to resonate inside her chest, like the bells of a church.—You want to prove yourself. And you're right, darling doll. Coming here, you *will*. You will gain friends, and popularity. I can't say your mother will be proud, but you don't really care about that right now, do you?

*It's true*, she thinks, forgetting her investigative purposes. *I want them to be impressed. And I want Mom to know I'm not like her…*

Shaky, Maju says yes. The smoke gets thicker. The fire is gone, excepting two candles. The room is completely black, until she looks up and sees the shadows on the wall. Cuca's smiling face is waxy and unnatural, her painted mouth looks robotic, her eyes glow oddly.

And there it is, the thing she has been looking for and has failed to find so far. Down Cuca's neck, she sees no double chin anymore, but a thick line that appears to be a scar. Squinting her eyes, Maju focuses on it, and finally notices the stitches.

– What did they tell you about me, little Maria Júlia?—Her

pink nail touches one of them, and the skin up her neck is wrinkling.—What do their silly rumors say?

– That... Um... That you have...—Maju gulps, because technically nothing is wrong, nothing but her vision. Behind Cuca, her shadow is elongating, like a very lengthy snout...—That you're much older than you look like...

– That much is true,—she cackles, and the lighting does not allow Maju to know for sure if her skin is changing color or not.—What else, baby? Tell Cuca.

– That you sold your soul to the devil.—Her guarana is bubbling more, and the table is trembling.—That you can go anywhere you want. Anywhere in time.

– Do you believe that?—The other's smile is arrogant, and makes her face look even more like a silicon mask.—Do you believe I can?

– I didn't,—she admits, and her palms are cold and sweaty. Maju feels like even if she wanted, she would not be able to run away.—I didn't before, but...

– You didn't before, and you wanted to come here to find proof, is that right? But things have changed.—A loud *bam* against the table, and the cowrie shells fall on the ground. Cuca is not mad, but now she stands up.—Skeptical little girl wanted to prove herself to her gullible little classmates, and sees now how wrong she was. Am I wrong, Maju? Tell me, I need to hear it from you.

Maju doesn't answer. She squeezes the arm of the chair, and looks at Cuca, unsure of what to say. The woman moves slowly to diminish the space between them, and holds the child by the chin.

– Tell me, Maju.

– I'm scared.—Her voice is but a whimper, and the confession makes Cuca laugh.

– Of course you are. But you don't need to be, doll.—The pointy part of Cuca's nail is scratching her skin, making a white line in the brown surface. Maju closes her eyes.—Many things people say about me are true, you see, but some are not... And I'm not one to hurt others that did nothing to me. Why would I hurt *you*?

Maja had thought her hand would feel cold, but Cuca's fingers are hot and alive, much unlike the image of her shadowed face.

– I don't know, ma'am.

– Then tell mama: what else did they tell you?—Maju feels a warm breath against her nose, and it is nothing human, like when her mother gives her kisses; it feels more like a hungry animal.—What do they say about my face?

– I... I...

– Stuttering won't get you any friends, Maju,—she advises softly, aware of how the girl's body is trembling from head to toe.—You have to talk clear and loud. Take this as a lesson for life... If you can't say it, open your eyes. Show you me you're brave, and I'll give you something great.

This time, she doesn't doubt. She opens her big brown eyes, glistering with candlelight, and raises her chin to face her.

Mama Cuca is still there, cigar in hand, blond hair falling over round shoulders, top and skirt, belly appearing, enormous in height and weight. The only difference between before and now is the head, since the skin mask is on the floor, and a crocodile with large yellow eyes is staring right at her.

– Ambition can take you to fantastic and horrifying places, little Maju.—Cuca's gigantic mouth is still grinning, displaying her sharp teeth. Her reptilian scales stop abruptly at the stitches of her neck, like someone had sewn them to her body with needle and thread.—I made my choice. Would you make yours? Do you want my help, or not?

Maju looks back at her, facing the black slit pupils, like a cat's.

– Yes. Yes, I do, Mama.

She hears a low, pleased chuckle. The alligator leers at Maju, and her human hands pull out a few strands of yellow hair, before tying it around the girl's wrist.

– Well, then. With this, you'll have what you want. If someone touches it, they'll have a glimpse of proof of what you have seen here. And when you're in need of help, you'll have a glimpse of my sight, too.

– But the payment…—Maju tries to get her backpack and the money she has in there. Cuca's hand is still tight around her arm.

– Listen to me, Maria Júlia Salles. Listen to me very carefully. *This,*—the nails again, now pulling the golden strand up to show the wristband,—is a gift. My prices are high, higher than you'd be able to even think. It's not only money that I take, it's much more than that. But I am giving it to you out of free will, because I was once a nosy little bug, just like you.—Maju agrees, never even blinking, afraid to lose eye contact.—Remember that. When no one did, Cuca liked you, Maria Júlia. So appreciate a small present for your curiosity and ambition. Understand?

– Yes!

Euphoric, Maju beams, vibrating with the words. The crocodile is not smiling anymore.

– Next time you need something, though…—Her voice echoes in the entire room, and a minor earthquake seems to start under her feet, the shadows moving swiftly across the walls. Cuca's yellow eyes gleam.—My price will be nowhere as moderate as the marketing I'm expecting you to do for me. Are we… understood?

– Yes! Yes, we are, Mama!

Everything stops. The soft breeze wafts the curtains into the room, and the windows are now open. All the candles have been extinguished, and the smoke is also gone. Cuca is back to her initial, average self.

– Good, then.—The woman smiles, appearing completely normal.—Great to do business with you. Jorge! Ricardo! Will you please show little miss Maju the exit?

Maju watches as Ricardo appears again, without any sign of being aware of abnormal activities inside the house.

– Thank you!—she bursts out, her ponytail bouncing at the sudden movement.—Mama Cuca, will I ever get to see you again?

Cuca stares at Ricardo and Jorge, both with a thoughtful and confused look. Then, the woman points to her own wrist.

– If we happen to not be in this town anymore, you can either use your gift, or try that little song your dad used to sing when you were a kid. What was it, again? *Sleep, baby...*

– *Or Cuca will get you...*—Maju sings too, the lullaby still fresh in her memory. Cuca laughs out loud.—Thank you again, Mama Cuca.

– Well, then. Farewell, little Maju. Ricardo, accompany the lady to the exit, and then bring me some cashew nuts and beer. It's about time to catch up with my TV shows.

Ricardo sighs, tired of the orders, but obeys anyway. He walks to the same door Maju entered an hour ago, and she runs after him. Her bicycle is still parked there, close to the palm tree. With her backpack hanging from one shoulder, she hops onto the seat and puts her violet helmet on. After leaving, she looks down at her new wristband, wondering exactly what will happen next.

# LATE ARRIVALS

## Tracy Townsend

Tracy Townsend teaches creative writing and sf/f literature at the Illinois Mathematics and Science Academy, a public boarding school for gifted students. She has two dogs and two children, but only one husband. If she's not teaching or writing, she's probably on Twitter (@TheStorymatic) being opinionated about books, comics, movies, and soup.

## 1.

When Mattie wakes to a scrubbed-clean kitchen and a pantry missing a can of stewed tomatoes and a box of chicken broth, she knows her mother has been making soup. Mom always makes soup Monday evenings. Mattie grew up living off a massive batch for a week at a time, a perilous admixture of leftover meats and vegetables rescued from the refrigerator's darkest corners. Once, Mom made a ragout of leftover fried rice and battered catfish. Anything can be combined, as far as she's concerned, with the power of a soup pot and stove.

Now, it's Tuesday morning, and the soup pot is burbling quietly, the fridge a little barer than before. Mattie supposes Mom's quest to save the previous week's leftovers might be comforting, if she hadn't already been dead for a year.

This isn't the first time she's come back to cook. It's the pot, Mattie figures. You can't separate a witch from her cauldron for long, yet no one in the family took Mattie seriously when she suggested putting the mustard- yellow Williams-Sonoma Dutch oven in the casket beside her mother. Mattie stared daggers at her father and grandmother, wanting to make them understand. Finally, Grandma muttered something about the enamel finish clashing with Mom's lavender funeral dress, and that had been the end of it.

The end for everyone else, anyway.

2.

The pot was a wedding gift, and probably didn't start out as a cauldron, but Mattie's mother came from a town of witches in Middle of Nowhere, Minnesota—a town peopled with the four-times-great-granddaughters of Welsh and Czech immigrants mixed up with the last of the Chippewa. If that couldn't stir up old magicks, nothing else would. The cauldron became Mattie's after Mom ended up in the nursing home with a fractured hip. On Christmas Eve, she buckled under the force of her third stroke as she climbed the kitchen stairs, and it had been a long, hard trip back down, once gravity had its say. Mom had all her words and her morbid streak back by St. Patrick's Day. Mattie came to visit on a Saturday around lunchtime, finding her mother bundled up in a wheelchair in the crowded dining hall, wedged between two residents half again her age. They ground the teeth they didn't have against rainbow-colored corned beef.

Between sullen forkfuls, Mom mentioned the cauldron.

"I can't use it now. It's yours."

Mattie hadn't lived at home for better than a decade. Still, she hadn't forgotten the cauldron or its almost-deadly soups, or the time the family dog had eaten a chicken carcass and slowly bled to death from the inside, swelling and moaning in agony. She was eleven at the time and had never seen anything die before. On the third night of the dog's suffering, Mom put an ear to its fluttering ribcage, stroked its muzzle, and said she knew something for pain. Out came the pot, warming leftover rice and broth and something strangely sweet unearthed from the back of a cabinet of loose-leaf teas. Mom gathered the shaggy spaniel in her lap to feed it dripping handfuls. She sang a long string of muttered nonsense, some kind of incantation, as the dog that hadn't eaten in three days wolfed and thumped its tail. An hour later, it was dead, but it had stopped moaning long before. Mom was still holding it, singing.

"I can't take that pot," Mattie answered, at last. "It's yours."

Mom turned her face away from another bite, grimacing. The corned beef leaked through the tines of the fork. They pureed her food now. "No, Mattie. It's the only thing of mine that matters. You should have it."

"You'll need it. You're going to be home in a week, back to poisoning Dad with your soup like always."

Mattie had said that three weeks running. Mom only nodded. They both knew she was never going home. They both knew neither of them was allowed to admit it.

"Still, you should stop by the house and take it home with you. Do it today."

"I will, Mom."

And Mattie knew she had three days—the time before her next visit—to invent a reason not to have made the trip. She was very good at finding excuses for a late arrival or a missed appointment. Her own magical gift. The thing she could always cook up.

### 3.

Dad remarried a woman who owned cookbooks and appreciated Food Network programming less than a year after Mom died. She also appreciated a tidy house, something which had always been a good deal lower on Mom's list of priorities. The basement was a storehouse of cracked eggshells, carefully washed and bagged; whole, dried musk melons with their centers inexplicably warded against rot; and the skeleton fingers of locust bean pods, stacked in plastic grocery bags and peeking from old Bell jars. A week after the honeymoon, it was transformed, neat as a pin, and Dad called Mattie to ask if she cared at all about the old Dutch oven.

"The enamel's cracked and the cast iron's rusting," he explained. Mattie could picture him rubbing the back of his neck as he spoke, his familiar gesture of awkward apology. "Arlene thinks it's not safe for cooking anymore, but I didn't think you'd want me to just –"

"I'll take it, Dad."

Mattie drove by that afternoon to take the pot back. At the door, she hugged her stepmother, who smelled of orange furniture polish, and had plans for the back garden to show off. She drove home an hour later with the pot cradled in her lap, iron all the way through and spilling over with guilt.

## 4.

Tuesday morning. The cauldron simmers on the stove, and the refrigerator no longer has a Tupperware bowl of pulled pork or two ears of corn stuffed in the back, because Mom is there, dead or not, standing by the coffee maker.

"I still haven't figured it out," she sighs when Mattie turns the corner into the fluorescent-bright kitchen.

"Haven't figured what out, Mom?"

"How I can work everything in the kitchen except your coffee maker. Is it on a timer or something?"

"It uses those little cup-things." Mattie points to a wire rack on a lazy Susan. "You just put them in and press the button."

"Really?" Mom brightens, digging around the carousel. A moment later, she has a cup going.

At least her hip doesn't seem to be bothering her, Mattie thinks. It's about the last thing that should occur to her. Why are you here? How are you here? Can you forgive me? Any of those should come first. All of those—the last, especially.

"Well," Mom breathes, shaking her head in wonder as the single-cup brewer sizzles. "Some things, I swear, are simply magic."

## 5.

Among the things Mom called "magic," before death and after:

Almond tea with milk.

Pussy willows.

Library book sales.

Dogs with blue eyes.

Cats with green eyes.

Wool socks.

Embroidery hoops.

Timeliness.

Mattie collects these things whenever she finds them. The last has proven the most elusive.

## 6.

Mom's health hadn't been great before the stroke and the broken hip. Migraine and liver problems. Anemia. The rolling blackouts of mini-seizures. Pain from fibromyalgia deep as a well and twice as dark. It had been bad enough already. Everything about the nursing home made it worse. Mom wouldn't eat, apart from the chocolate pudding the orderlies used to feed her round after round of Relpax and Keppra and heparin. By April, her charts clearly indicated she was to have a thin liquids diet only. She only wanted grilled cheese sandwiches and tomato soup.

Mahmoud, her mid-week attendant, insisted both were strictly off limits.

Mattie smuggled in stacks of sandwiches wrapped in waxed paper and an old steel Thermos of soup each time she visited. Feeding Mom was equal parts ritual and sin, and not just because the food was forbidden.

Mom would drink her soup and sigh in ecstasy, her sallow face finally relaxed. "You heated it in the pot. I can tell. It tastes just like it should."

In an undergraduate ethics class, a professor had lectured Mattie on lies of omission, though she'd already been well-practiced in them. She nodded.

"I'm glad you like it."

On Tuesday nights, Mattie had a yoga class. That always threw off her visiting schedule. Mattie would creep in at seven o'clock, Mom's room long since dark behind heavy drapes, and find her mother already fast asleep. She kept a notebook in her purse, but the pages never tore out right. She'd leave messages scrawled on the backs of receipts, instead.

I hid the soup between your mattress and the bed rail. Give Dad the Thermos when he visits tomorrow. I'll get it back from him later.

Mattie always meant to add, "I miss you," but stopped short. It would be cruel—a kind of accusation. Mom hadn't asked for something to stir the chemicals in her brain wrong and leave her in an ugly stew.

I'll see you Saturday morning, she'd finish instead.

She would arrive in the mid-afternoon.

### 7.

"I thought writers sleep slept in," Mom says, stirring her coffee cup. She stands on the opposite side of the kitchen island. Mattie takes the sight of her in with slow blinks, frame by frame.

"Some, maybe. I heard something on the baby monitor. I thought it was Kathy."

"Mmmm." The sound is the taste of coffee and the acknowledgement of fact. "Is she sleeping through the night yet?"

The question stings Mattie's eyes. "You should go upstairs and see for yourself," she whispers.

## 8.

Mattie and Mom were both wrong. She left the nursing home, after all, but not to go home. The doctors knew what they were looking at, and so they told Mattie's father it was time for his wife to see anyone who was important to her—to go back to her family.

After that, Mom spent three weeks in hospice care, bustled over by her husband, her octogenarian mother, and two nurses on shifts. She lay on the same mattress in the same bed in the same cottage by a Minnesota lake that had been her childhood home. Mattie intended to replace her three thrice-weekly visits with three phone calls, but you'd have thought the phone had burst into flames and thorns, as often as she picked it up.

Late on a Saturday afternoon, six months pregnant and finishing the paint in the nursery, Mattie saw her phone ring, the screen lighting up with a picture of her grandmother's face.

"Come... here," the old woman sobbed. "There's not much time."

It was a twelve- hour drive to the Minnesota lake house. She didn't even take the time to close the cans of paint.

Mattie stuffed two days of clothes, a black maternity dress, and a string of pearls into a duffel bag. She poured tea into a Thermos. By dusk, her tiny orange hatchback was pelting north, a blur of fog lights and blaring radio. Just outside of St. Paul, she veered west around Lake Vadnais when she ought to have gone east and didn't realize her mistake for thirty minutes. She had to backtrack through long trenches of construction and lane closures for better than an hour before she had her bearings again.

Just outside of Owens, Mattie's phone buzzed.

Her grandmother's quavering voice. News. Questions. Stupidly, Mattie nodded her answers, then closed the call.

She was still an hour away. Lost-at-Vadnais Lake-away. The baby jammed a foot between her ribs and pushed until Mattie thought she would split at her seams.

Mattie arrived just in time to help the funeral home attendant load the gray, silent form that had been her mother onto a gurney. She stood beside her duffel bag and watched the hearse's tail lights disappear down the winding gravel lane. She slept in her mother's bed that night. There were only three in the house, and she thought it would be wrong for her father or grandmother to have to take it—to lie right there, where the woman they'd loved had died.

Mattie crowded her half-moon body to the farthest edge of the mattress, reaching to the opposite pillow, tracing the topsheet's hem. Her mother's warmth was long gone, but the sheets still smelled of her—stale and rumpled and familiar.

Mattie had weeks of conversations stored up. By dawn, the bed knew her as well as anyone.

### 9.

Kathy was born in the middle of August. Mom had died in May. Passing ships in the night, a friend said consolingly.

Mattie wanted to punch him in the neck.

Kathy hadn't wanted for her tiny, leaf-shaped ship to sail past her grandmother's. She was born wild and fierce. Only hours old, she had a wry smile so much like Mom's, Mattie shivered when she caught it out of the corner of her eye. Kathy had wanted so badly not to miss her grandmother—not to come into the world trailing in her wake—that she was born with less than two hours' labor, practically in the hospital parking lot, screaming even before her body had passed completely into the world.

There'd been no time for an epidural or much of anything else. Mattie was still half in her street clothes. As she lolled her head to spy the squalling, purple-brown infant kicking in rage, she knew in her bones being a witch must skip a generation.

That first night in the nursery wing, neither of them slept, but Kathy was already done crying. She stared at Mattie, her blurry, just-born face demanding answers. If there had been something to omit, Mattie might have found the right lie, but Kathy was a hungry black hole, eyes tirelessly pulling at her.

"You were late before you started, honey," Mattie whispered, over and over. "I'm sorry."

Eventually, Kathy turned her face toward the dim outline of the door, studying it with eyes like pools of ink. Mattie watched it with her. Outside, nurses shuffled quietly between rooms, delivering newborns to mothers who didn't know how to nurse them, taking orders from fathers who didn't know how to help. Every time footsteps came near or slowed, Mattie was sure the door would open, and she'd see Mom on the other side.

The whole night passed, and then the morning, and Mom never came through the door.

Mattie supposed that was reasonable. Mom had never been late for anything in her life, it was true. But now she was dead. It seemed an unfair expectation.

Six months later, Mattie came home from her father and step-mother's house, put the cauldron on her kitchen counter, and stood for an hour staring into its empty landscape, cratered like the moon.

10.

Being a witch must skip a generation, because Mattie's grandmother is about as magical as a doorknob, and Mattie could be the doorstop to go with it. She has never doubted what Mom was. The evidence was too clear.

Once, on the drive back from an archdiocese potluck, Mom brought her Impala station wagon to a screeching halt and bolted toward a knot of people tying up the middle of the road. Mattie jerked around in her seat in time to see her mother push through the crowd, gathered around a man who'd been thrown from his motorcycle. She lost sight of her mother when she kneeled down beside the crimson mess and called for towels. No helmet, and now no back to the rider's head. Mom wrapped him with her muttering voice and bloody, homemade turbans. Mattie sat alone in the car, the half-full potluck cauldron on the floorboards garlicky and pungent, holding a congealed something her mother had had the audacity to tell Father Michael was "a gumbo." It made her stomach turn.

"Mattie!" Mom's voice was so shrill, Mattie had hardly recognized it. "Mattie—bring the pot!"

The pot was heavy enough empty. Half-full, Mattie had to brace it against her hip and lug it ahead with big, stumbling steps. The lid rattled, threatening to topple off. She paused just outside the parting ring of bystanders. Through the trunks of legs, Mattie could see smears of red, and maybe something else, something thick and—

"Just leave it there, sweetheart," Mom said over her shoulder. "I'll be done in a minute. Go back to the car."

And Mattie had nodded and skittered like a teacup dog. Vanishingly far, she heard her mother asked someone else to open the pot. Mattie she lay flat on her back in the Impala's backseat, staring at the saggy fabric ceiling so she couldn't peek out the windows. The car still reeked of sausages and garlic. The street did, too, now.

When the ambulance came ten minutes later, the man was still alive, and well enough a month after to send my guardian angel, Kathy a thank-you card in his own, wobbly hand.

At thirteen, Mattie lost her retainer down the toilet and spent a day planning the lies she'd have to tell to keep out of trouble. When her mother came home from third shift at the hospital and found Mattie sitting awake on the couch, waiting, she said nothing. Mom went to the kitchen, pulled the cauldron from its cabinet, and lifted its lid.

The retainer was inside.

"It's unbelievable where I lose things, sometimes, honey. You look pale. You should go to bed."

The summer her family went to Mackinac Island, Mattie's half-blind next door neighbor was left in charge of feeding and watering the family gerbils. The woman couldn't see that after a few days, the water feeder had gone dry. Desert animals, she explained tearfully. I thought they must not need to drink very much.

Mattie came home to a pack of pups nursing at their mother's desiccated corpse, chirruping and wriggling with the last of their strength. She was only nine, but she knew a dead thing when she saw it. The mother gerbil looked like a bit of windblown roadkill.

Mom took the musty, brittle corpse from the aquarium and tutted softly. "Well! You, lady, are in need of a bath. Phew!"

Mattie knew better than to ask questions of her mother.

Mom gave the gerbil a bath in her cauldron-pot, Dad scowling over her shoulder the whole time.

"That's a dead rodent, Kathy. You can't honestly expect us to eat stuff that comes out of that thing aga—"

The gerbil squeaked and shuddered, jerking up from a dream. Mom gathered it up in a dishtowel and carried it back to the aquarium.

"I most certainly do," she said. And they did.

11.

Here's the thing about magic.

You will know it when you see it. Perhaps it will be your own doing, and you'll be the force that opens the door, not some dull piece of hardware bolted on it. You can live your life surrounded by magic, though, without learning to cast a single spell.

Mattie's life is like that. Mom first. Now Kathy. Kathy's not yet a year old, but she walks with tottering determination, solid as a golem, and things Mattie can't explain happen around her all the time. But Mattie grew up without explanations. She had her mother's soup and tea and embroidery hoops, instead—though never her sense of timeliness.

Not yet a year old, Kathy is wound more precisely than any clock.

She wakes at five-thirty every morning, the sky already growing light. Somehow, Mattie knows that if Mom wants to see her, she'll have to do it now. It comes down to the timing. Seeing the moment of need and answering it.

Mattie stands in the nursery doorway, watching sunlight burn through Mom's silver hair as she walks, slow and unsteady, to the rail of Kathy's crib.

The child lies on her back, an arm thrown above her head, Cupid's bow lips parted. Her breath is milk and heat. Mom reaches down, rests a thin, blue-veined hand on the curve of her cheek. That's when Mattie blinks away a tear.

Somewhere in that flickering moment, Mom is gone, and Kathy's eyes open.

Five-thirty. Perfect timing.

She stretches and yawns, her tiny mouth a scarlet "O."

## 12.

Mattie's husband doesn't ask why she made soup in the middle of the night, and doesn't complain about how awful it is. He's learned some questions are better left alone—learned to recognize when he's come into the room a moment too late for answers to matter.

There's enough in the pot to last the whole week. On the following Monday night, Mattie leaves it on the stove with a wooden spoon, scrubbed clean. She lies in bed all night, staring at the ceiling.

There's no soup in the morning, but there is a note on the back of a grocery store receipt.

# ROPES OF WHITE BONE, WINGS OF DARK MAGIC

## Meryl Stenhouse

Meryl Stenhouse lives in subtropical Queensland where she curates an extensive notebook collection and fights a running battle with the Lego models trying to take over the house. When not avoiding stealth bricks she can be found at the computer, avoiding writing. She has no writing qualifications other than experience, cynicism and an outdated science degree.

The high-pitched scream of a dragon echoed across the swamp. Lilka leaped to her feet, sending her meal into the fire. She ran to her drake, grabbed the nose ring and hauled his head down, choking off his answering cry.

A full squad of nine dragons flew over them, high up in the wispy autumn clouds.

Lilka watched until the dragons disappeared from view to the north, all the while keeping a firm grip on Corion's nose ring.

"All right, they're gone." She scratched under his jaw. "Settle down. No point getting huffy my lad, they'd make a quick meal out of you." Corion snorted, washing her with his warm carrion breath. Barely larger than a draught horse, the drake was a third of the size of the big war dragons.

Lilka soothed him and then checked his wing, where a long scar marred the smooth, cold hide. No heat, no pus, but the area was tender and Corion pulled away from her hands.

The afternoon sun painted the narrow channels in blood, and tipped every reed with fire. Lilka stared out across the swamp. Too often now the flights of dragons would pass over. How soon until one of them swooped low and spotted her hiding place?

She chewed at her lip. Corion's wing was healed enough.

They would have to fly, try to get back to their own side. How far, though? How far had Matten advanced in the two months she had been here? Corion snorted and she glanced up in alarm, but the skies were empty. She dared not stay longer.

Lilka spent the evening dismantling her camp, one eye on the skies, ready to run for the thicket where Corion was concealed. She scattered reeds and brush over the bare ground and dragged her gear under the tangled branches. She packed her saddlebags and hung them over a tree branch.

As she did every night, she pulled out the short-bristled brushes and rough cloth from her kit, and brushed and buffed the drake's hide until it shone. She checked the wing again. Tomorrow. Just one more night. Tomorrow they would fly.

At midnight the snap and crack of Corion's tether woke her and she was glad she had tied the drake's head down. Above them the stars winked in and out as flight after flight of dragons passed overhead. There must have been well over a hundred. Lilka leaned into Corion's neck as the drake fussed and fussed.

No-one had guessed what Matten, the strange new king from the northern countries, had been breeding in his cold stone halls. No rumours had escaped to warn her country of what was coming. Dragons. How? How had he controlled them, trained them, brought these ancient creatures of magic to his army?

Lilka closed her eyes and shuddered. Her squad had been doing a sweep along the border. Nights spent in camp under the stars with men and women who were her friends as well as her peers. How could they have known what waited for them? Madness. Madness. Tumbling, screaming, the crunch of bone and the beat of wings. Flying home before the invaders, warning the outpost but too late, too late to save anyone.

Lilka opened her eyes again so she wouldn't see the images in her mind. When the retreat was called she had lost sight of her companions in the dark. She didn't know if they had survived. She and Corion had limped away into the night while behind her the outpost burned.

Corion grumbled and rubbed his jaw along the ground. Up above, the stars shone unimpeded and to the north, a hundred dragons flew on. How far would they go? How much resistance would the dragons meet before they reached the capitol and the great hall of the senate? And in between, her village, the old brown house with the creaky stairs and her mother who always smelled of cinnamon cake and soap.

After the dragons would come the foot soldiers, the support for the great army machine. Her swamp was no longer safe.

She harnessed Corion in the darkness, placing straps by familiarity and touch. At the first hint of dawn, she led the drake out of the thicket. Mist rose in pale fingers from the dark channels, and over to the east a lonely bird cried in the day. She rubbed a hand over Corion's nose, spoke reassuring nonsense to him, then stepped back.

"Up!" she cried. Corion shuffled his half-spread wings, tensed, every movement one of uncertainty. Lilka's heart sank.

"Come on. Just give it a try." That was no good. She stepped closer, stood right in his view. "Up!" She flung up one arm to reinforce the command. Corion crouched on powerful legs, then thrust himself into the air. His wings spread and Lilka held her breath for that split-second moment before the first powerful downstroke swept him into flight.

One cry of pain, but he was flying! She whistled at him to circle, watching critically from below. The wing beats were short, that was obvious, but he had enough movement there to keep himself in the air.

She whistled him down and he back-winged, claws digging into the mud. She rubbed his jaw, made a fuss, wished she had some fresh meat to give him. The wing seemed fine when she checked it, trembling, but not hot. He wouldn't manage a long flight;, they would have to do it in stages. But he could fly. Finally, they were going home.

Lilka ran to the thicket for her sack. As she bent to grab it, she saw Corion stiffen.

"No!" She dashed forward, but was too slow. He reared, flung his head back and bellowed a challenge to the sky. She grabbed the halter and hauled him down, but the damage had been done.

High above, three dark shapes banked and turned. Lilka threw herself onto Corion's back, felt him dance beneath her, bubbling with fight.

"Up!" she cried.

Corion crouched, then launched himself into the air. For a moment the ground tilted at a crazy angle, and then his wing beats steadied and they surged upwards. She guided him low over the trees, glanced behind her, saw the massive dragons arrowing down towards them.

Ahead was all scrub, with narrow channels between the reeds, and the distant glint of a lake. Nowhere to hide. A low dark line to the east might be forest and she urged Corion in that direction. He turned poorly, already tiring. Too much, too fast, for a recently healed wing.

Then the dragons were on them, great beasts dwarfing them both, riders faceless behind goggles and scarves. Lilka tensed and cried out, waiting for the grip of talons, the sharp bite of a spear.

But no pain came. The three dragons crowded in, forcing them east around the lake. Corion bellowed, fought for control. She tried to duck away under them, but Corion's wings beat three times for every one of theirs. He moaned, his ribs between her calves heaving with effort.

Then they were over land and he was struggling, pulling short, losing height and they tumbled down and slammed into the mud.

Dazed, Lilka struggled to her feet, her mind full of teeth and talons and faceless enemies. Pain exploded up her back, her ribs, and then she was soaring up, away from the ground, arms and legs dangling and a vice around her chest.

She screamed. Below her, Corion struggled in the grip of another dragon. The wind buffeted her, icy and deafening, and louder still the rhythmic thump and slap of the great wings.

Fields swung below her, patchwork greens and browns, toy houses, growing smaller. Then blackened patches and hollow shells of villages and she shuddered. The cold ate at her, seeped into her bones. Time dragged and she grew woozy with motion sickness, like a rookie on their first flight. She vomited, retching until her belly was empty. Then they banked, pushing her ribs painfully against the iron talons.

Below and to the right she saw grey stone buildings. The dragons back-winged and her vision went black. She came to as they thumped into the ground.

The talons opened and she tumbled onto the dirt. Someone hauled her to her feet. She realised she was surrounded by soldiers, pale men in uniforms slashed with red. They dragged her, stumbling and shaking, to a door and hurled her through. She landed on her knees. The sickly smell of decaying flesh overwhelmed her and she retched onto the dank straw beneath her.

A pair of dirty boots appeared in her vision.

"Welcome to Jurien internment camp, soldier."

The words made no sense. Jurien was a farming community.

Her patrol had been through there many times. She tried to stand, stumbled down again. This was all wrong.

***

Hedersen, the one-armed sergeant, was from Teres. Vander with the missing eye was from Barrenan. No-one knew where the man with the charred and festering skin came from. He died the first night Lilka spent at the camp.

Two men carried him out to the edge of the fields to bury him, under the watchful eyes of the soldiers. Lilka sat with her back against the rough stone wall of the barn. Her stomach refused to keep food down, between the lingering smell of the dead soldier and her own aching ribs and head.

Occasionally she would hear Corion calling to her. She wiped her eyes. The two of them had not been apart since she had been accepted into the scout wing. Corion, newly hatched and untrained, had been such a handful to a young private barely out of her teens. But they had learned together, lived together for so long, his absence was painful. He wanted food, he wanted attention, he wanted her. She wanted nothing more than to fling herself on his back and fly away.

Hedersen came over to her.

"How are you feeling this morning?"

"Fine, sir."

He grunted as he sat down beside her.

"What happened to the village, sir?"

"No, idea. It was like this when I came."

"When was that?"

"Two weeks ago. But I won't be here much longer. They clear the camp out every month or so, or when it gets too full."

"How do you know?"

"Because that's what they told me when I got here." He shuffled around to a more comfortable position. "Listen up, because now you get to hear the spiel too. Everyone does, and hopefully someone will get the information we have back over the line."

"What information?"

Hedersen jerked his head in the direction of the door. "The dragons."

Lilka shivered, and clenched her hands together to stop them trembling. "What about them?"

"We think——" He glanced at the door, lowered his voice. "We're pretty sure they're controlled by magic."

Lilka's head snapped up. "What?"

"Shh!"

She lowered her voice to a whisper. "It can't be. Not even Matten would use magic." She swallowed bile at the word, then saw the look on Hederson's face. "Would he?"

"Hah." Hedersen stood. "You come with me." He led her over to the ladder up to the loft. The climb hurt her, and she had to pause for a moment at the top.

"Over here."

She followed him to one of the narrow slits high in the wall. There was a prisoner stationed at each one, watching.

Hedersen nodded to the thin man peering through the gap. He stepped back, limping, and Lilka saw the bloody bandage on his thigh.

Hedersen pointed to the left. "Look."

She leaned forward and peered out. In the yard, sentries followed their circuit between the barn and the drystone wall. On the other side of the wall, cows grazed.

"What am I supposed to see?"

"Look! To the left, near the gate."

She shifted until she could see the gate, and then she saw what Hedersen wanted her to see.

Three men sat in a circle around a low fire. Each wore a heavy circlet of metal. Around them, six slender poles were arranged in a regular pattern. Between the poles hung ropes strung with odd, pale objects that she couldn't identify. Then the wind rose, rattling the objects against each other and she realised they were bones.

She thrust herself back from the window and tumbled into the straw. "No."

"Yes." Hedersen crouched down beside her.

She looked up at him, still not willing to believe, not willing to accept that anyone, any human, would be so depraved as to perform magic.

"Come on." He held out a hand to help her up.

Lilka followed him back down the ladder, slowly because her hands were still shaking and her gut rolling worse than ever. At the bottom she leaned her head on the ladder and closed her eyes.

"Pull yourself together, private."

"Yes, sir." She swallowed. Had they dug those bones up from a grave, she wondered, or had they chopped someone up like a carcass?

She went down on her knees in the straw and vomited, thankful that her belly was already empty. Hedersen stepped back until she was done.

"Now you know," he said as she wiped her mouth on her sleeve. "Those—"

The door was flung open and everyone turned. A group of filthy, bloody men were herded through and the door slammed behind them.

Hedersen strode over to them, other soldiers at his heels and the newcomers were assisted to the corner where the injured lay on blankets over straw. Lilka pushed herself to her feet and went to see if she could help. Someone shoved a bucket at her. "Water!"

"Where?"

"I'll show you." Vander, the soldier with the missing eye, grabbed another bucket. "Follow me." He walked over to the door and knocked on it.

"What is it?" came through the door.

"We need water."

There was the sound of the bar being lifted and the door swung open. Lilka followed Vander through the door, past a pair of guards.

Vander led her across the yard to the pump, and her heart lifted. Aside from the soldiers on the door, she could see only four sentries, the pair doing the circuit around the barn, and the pair on the gate. Beyond them the fields were open, and on the other side of the fields was the edge of a wood.

"Is this all the soldiers?" she asked Vander as they bent over the pump. "It doesn't look well-guarded."

"Look up," he said.

She looked. Overhead, three dragons flew in lazy circles. "Oh."

"You're not the first to think about trying it. Ask Hedersen about what happened to the soldiers who made a run for it."

The image of bones in the wind filled her mind and she pushed it away.

They filled the buckets and returned under the watchful eyes of the sentries. She deposited her bucket near the injured soldiers, but there was nothing else for her to do. Hedersen was deep in conversation with a group of men including one of the newcomers. Vander moved over to join them and she followed.

"—came over the hills. No idea they could fly that high. They were into the city before we realised."

City? "Which city?" she asked.

"Koongal."

"But that's—"

"Quiet!" snapped Hedersen. "Go on."

"We were expecting them to come around, come at the city from the south. We had scouts out as soon as we heard that Glen Moore had fallen. They said we'd have three days to prepare. We had about three3 hours. There weren't even any refugees on the road. They started coming after the battle. It was all over so fast."

Lilka's heart hammered in her chest and she turned away to hide her tears. Koongal was in the heartlands, a great, bright city of flowing banners and many thousands of people. And between there and here was her little village. She closed her eyes. Her mother, her brother. Dead? Or on the road, with thousands of other refugees, looking for food and shelter as winter crept nearer? She realised that the newcomer was still talking, and wiped her eyes.

"—was three days ago. We got separated, rode down across the lowlands, hoping to get to the port, which was still free last we heard. But they caught us in open country just north of here."

Hedersen grabbed the man by the arm. "Did you see any posts on your way through?"

"Posts?"

"Groups of six, with men in the middle."

The man shook his head. "No, nothing. We didn't even see any foot soldiers until about a day later."

"No foot soldiers in the invasion?"

"No. The dragons came in, slaughtered the main defense and dropped men straight into the middle of the city. There were hundreds of them. We barely killed a score with the ballista."

"I saw them." The words came out without thinking, and suddenly Lilka was the centre of attention.

"Where?"

"In the swamplands, south of Wandal. They flew over, two nights ago."

"Couldn't be. We were attacked three days ago."

"Which means there's another wing out there somewhere."

In the horrified silence, they could hear the moans of one of the injured men.

"We have to get this information back." Hedersen slammed his fist against his thigh.

"How?" Vander stepped into the circle. "I'm not keen on ending my days as dragon food."

"Doesn't matter. If we don't get this information back to the defenses—"

"Then what?" An injured soldier pushed in, angrily. "We've already lost. If they can get from Glen Moore to Koongal in a day, how are we supposed to defeat them?"

"We have to let people know about the—" he lowered his voice. "About the magic. It's all we've got."

"What magic?"

"Come with me, and I'll explain."

Lilka left them to it. She leaned against the wall, slid down it. Hedersen was right, but so was the injured soldier. They had lost. They had nothing that could defeat the great beasts, the mass of Matten's army.

\*\*\*

They slept in shifts that night. Some soldiers on duty to warn if the enemy came too near the doors, others resting. Still others sat in a tight group in the centre of the barn, plotting in whispers.

Lilka found herself in that group. She knew why. Hedersen had ideas of her flying off on Corion. She was in favour of that idea in theory, but every time she thought about it, she remembered three great shadows forcing them down into the mud, claws slamming into her, dragging her through the whirling sky.

Hedersen's voice was not made for whispering. Instead he produced a muted roar that Lilka was sure would carry out the door. "We just need to distract the dragons long enough for Lilka to get range."

"By being eaten?" Lilka shifted on the coarse straw.

"Look, it's risky, but it's the only way."

"They can outpace me."

"Not if they don't see where you go." Vander leaned forward. "I say we set the barn on fire."

Lilka looked away. It didn't matter what they did on the ground. She didn't want to get into the sky with those dragons. Not again.

"And how come she gets to ride, anyway? Why don't we draw lots, give everyone a chance?" The speaker, Ferris, was one of the new soldiers.

Lilka shook her head. "Corion won't let anyone else ride him."

"She's right. Scout drakes only have one rider." Vander smiled at her.

"Can't be that hard."

Vander snorted. "He's not a horse. Anyway, you're too heavy."

Ferris opened his mouth to argue.

"Enough." Hedersen's scowl chastised them all. "Lilka flies, and that's the end of it. Now we need to get her far enough ahead that she can make it to Beacon's Field."

"Assuming they haven't taken it already."

"If they have, we're done for anyway. That's the last defense before the heartlands."

"They might have gone around it."

"And they might have given up and gone home! We can't know. We can only work on what we've got. Lilka rides—"

"Sentry!" hissed one of the watchers. They fell silent until the watcher gave the all clear.

"Lilka rides to Beacon's Field. We distract the guards and the dragons as long as we can to give her a start."

"She'll never make it."

Lilka privately agreed, but Hedersen's glare was enough to silence them.

"Any more gripes?"

"Other than I don't want to die?" Vander grinned at Hedersen, mimed fending him off.

"Fine. Get some sleep, and prepare yourselves. We see a chance tomorrow, we're going for it."

They settled down into the straw. Lilka rolled to one side, her mouth dry. She closed her eyes, tried to sleep. The tread of the sentries as they circled the barn echoed in her head. What was the point of fearing the dragons, when there were men with swords outside? She got up and went to the bucket for a drink.

When she came back, Vander was propped up on one elbow, a dim shape in the gloom.

"Nervous?"

"Yes." She hesitated, then sat down next to him. "How did you know about scout drakes?"

Vander pushed up to a sitting position. "I started in scouts. Years ago. But I got too heavy, so they moved me to signals. Now I spend my days mixing chemicals and trying not to blow up my company."

Lilka smiled. "You don't ride anymore?"

"Only horses. I thought I could stick with the corps, be a trainer, but it was too painful, seeing everyone else flying. Better to get right away."

"I guess." She wasn't dreaming about flying now.

"So where's your family?"

"Farley." She looked up and caught his eye.

"I'm sorry." His hand, warm, gripped hers.

"What about your family?" Her voice sounded rough and she cleared her throat.

"Oh, there's just me. My father died just before I went into service, my mother soon after."

"Vander—"

"It's all right. It was a long time ago."

"A long time?"

"Well, it feels like it." He smiled and then she noticed the laughter lines around his eyes.

"How did you get here?"

Vander shrugged. "I survived." He looked away. "I suppose I was lucky."

"We're going to die tomorrow, aren't we?"

He turned to her, face solemn. "Maybe." Then a smile broke

out. "But what's life without adventure?" The smile faded when he saw her expression. "Sorry." He squeezed her hand.

"I don't want this to be the end."

"I think the end is already here. We've got—" He shook his head. "We've got nothing against this army. Not when they can swoop across the land faster than we can defend."

Lilka turned away. She didn't want to think about life under Matten's rule. Matten with his dark history, iron rule, whispers of slavery and who knew what else. Would there be ropes of bone strung over the villages?

She hugged her knees to her chest. "If we get this information back, they might be able to help. Strike in the right places."

"Maybe."

"You don't believe it."

Vander shrugged, gave her a half smile. "You keep hoping, Lilka. And no matter what happens, there's a good chance you'll get home."

"To what?"

"Don't think about that. Look too far ahead and you can see the darkness coming." He lay down. "Go to bed. Try to sleep. It will all be over tomorrow."

Lilka nodded and returned to her place. She caught a glimpse of pale eyes in the gloom, someone else who couldn't sleep. As she passed, she realised it was Ferris. She smiled at him but he rolled onto his side, away from her.

In the morning, faces were drawn and pale, jaws tense, eyes downcast. Most of these men would die today if they went ahead with the plan. The thought made Lilka gag, and she hurried to the water bucket, gulped down the tepid liquid.

"All right there, Lilka?"

She wiped her mouth and turned to face Hedersen. "Yes, sir." The bile bubbled up in her throat and she choked.

Hedersen stepped forward and grabbed her arm, his fingers digging in until she cried out.

"Don't you dare!" he hissed. He hauled her over to the wall. "Pull yourself together, soldier!"

"I'm not—" His fingers dug in harder and she gasped. "We can't do this. They'll die. Those dragons—" Tears dampened her cheeks.

"Stop it." He shook her, and she tried to gulp back her tears. "Maybe we will. But the only reason these men have the courage to go out there and face things is because they know that you will get that information back to the people who can do something about it. Do you hear me? If you give up, you're spitting in the face of these men."

"I don't want anyone to die."

"People are already dying. And a lot more will die if we don't stop this. You want these people ruling us? You want your family to live in a village with dragons on the hills and bones rattling in the wind?"

"No."

"Then you'd better put everything you've got into today, because this might be our country's last chance. Look at me."

She raised her head to meet his gaze. Brown eyes, and a scar under his fringe that she hadn't noticed before.

"Are you going to make it, scout?"

She took a deep breath. "Yes, sir."

"Good soldier." He let her go. Her fingers started to tingle and she realised he had been gripping her arm hard enough to cut off the circulation. He strode off, calling to the men in a low voice. Everyone who could stand was to play their part.

Lilka rubbed her arm. She had said she would do it, but she wondered, when it came to the time, if she would be able to run across that field under those dragons and onto Corion's back.

She had to stop thinking about it. While the men prepared, she climbed up into the loft to the narrow window. Corion was still calling to her.

Someone hissed her name and she turned to see Vander at the top of the ladder.

"You're wanted."

She almost fell down the ladder on shaking legs. Vander led her to Hedersen, standing by the water buckets.

"Ready?"

There was only one answer. "Yes, sir."

Hedersen banged on the door. "Water!"

Lilka held her breath. Men waited on either side of the door as it opened to let Hedersen and Vander out. The two stepped between the soldiers and then the men charged, forcing the doors wide.

The guards went down in the scuffle, and the opening was clear. But Lilka couldn't move, couldn't breathe. Go. Go now! she told her unresponsive body.

Then Vander was beside her, blood running down his arm. She ran forward into the sunlight. Hedersen and another soldier charged alongside them.

Corion bellowed from the other side of the yard. Between them was a melee of soldiers and guards.

She heard the thump and crack of wings and froze.

Vander grabbed her and dragged her into the melee and then they were charging across the yard, a wedge of men around her, not stopping for the guards running towards them, all intent on Corion. A shadow swept over them.

"Scatter!" shouted Hedersen. She doveived to the side and there was a thump and screams and she spat out dirt. She rolled and scrambled away, sobbing, smelling blood in the air. Corion screamed and she concentrated on him. She stumbled over a body, heard something snap behind her but she didn't stop to look.

She scrambled over the low wall to Corion, pulling frantically at the chain around his neck. With fumbling fingers she tried to unclip the hook but he pulled it out of her hands. Unthinking, she looked behind her.

A dragon filled the yard, wings unfurled, ground bloody and torn beneath its feet. It plucked a soldier up in its jaws and she watched, unable to look away, as the soldier tumbled down in pieces.

Then Hedersen was running, under the great neck and across the yard and she screamed as it saw him and the horned head turned. But then he was among the wizards. A sword flashed up and one of them fell into the fire.

The dragon screamed and reared and the guards dropped their weapons and fled. She saw the rider tossed high into the air.

She turned away, screaming at Corion to be still, and then the latch was undone and the chain fell to the ground. She grabbed for his neck harness and hauled herself up.

Something grabbed her foot and slammed her into the dirt. She looked up to see Ferris dive at Corion and haul himself onto the drake's back. He kicked the drake in the ribs, shouted at him to fly. Corion reared and Ferris tumbled to the dirt.

Lilka ran around him and grabbed the drake's halter. Corion

rolled his eyes and backed away from her. She pulled herself up onto his back.

The soldier grabbed her leg and she kicked out. Corion danced away, wings up. Ferris stumbled after them.

"Take me too!" he cried.

"I can't!" She turned away from his face, swallowed a sob and commanded Corion to take wing.

They leaped upwards. Lilka looked back, wind lashing her face and drawing tears. Through a film of water she saw the soldiers and guards fleeing into buildings as the uncontrolled dragon rampaged through them. Guilt squirrelled in her guts and she urged Corion on.

It was difficult to fly without her goggles. She could only guide Corion in the general direction and hope that she could keep him on track. Every time she recognised a land-mark, she corrected their path.

Below her the forest gave way to farmland and her chest constricted. But the buildings were undisturbed. Men carried loads or worked the soil and beasts fed in peace in the fields. The normality shocked her. Had the war passed this area by? Hope rose for her family and her little village.

Instinctively she urged Corion to the right. In a few minutes she found the eastern highway, one of the great roads that led into the heart of their country. If she followed this for an hour, she would come to the low hill country and the massive fortification of Beacon's Field.

The illusion of normalcy didn't last. Small groups appeared on the road, one or two, then a dozen, then more. Families with wagons and oxen, or on foot. Displaced people moving to the edge of the country, not to its heart. Matten's army had cut into them, split the country in two, and these people were now in enemy territory.

Ahead she saw the outline of a large town and she veered to

go around it. Too late she saw the poles at the gate. She urged Corion away, looking behind her for the shape of a dragon launching into the air.

Corion stiffened beneath her and she nearly lost her seat as he ducked to the left, crying out in pain. Then she heard the snap of wings and the shadow of a dragon passed over her.

Terror blinded her and she screamed, driving Corion down towards the trees, waiting for the talons. The drake fought her, pulling them up just before the trees scraped his belly.

The dragon drove them towards the town and Lilka now saw the camps with their foreign flags flying. Defeat washed over her. She hadn't tried hard enough. She saw the ring of mages ahead of her. More bones rattling in the wind.

Courage she didn't realise she possessed bubbled up and she urged Corion down, sweeping straight for the mages and their vile circle. They heard Corion's scream and leaped up, scattering the fire as she charged through. The ropes with their clattering bones caught around Corion's neck, trailing after them as they soared upwards.

Behind her the dragon roared and she risked a look. It flung its great neck up, tossing its rider like a doll. The man hung on as the beast doveied.

Lilka urged Corion away towards Beacon's Field. Five more minutes and they would be there. She felt lighter. Hedersen had been right. This information could save them.

She heard the scream of a dragon and looked behind. Its rider was gone, but the dragon was still after them. Corion needed no urging. The tired drake put on a burst of speed, and she felt him trembling between her calves. Every time she looked back, the dragon was closer.

Ahead the low, dark line of a fortification rose. She burst out over the field and saw below her a massed army of foot soldiers in gold and red. Matten's army had caught up with the dragons.

Something whistled by her and she ducked. Then she saw the men around the ballistae on the walls. They were shooting at her! No, they were shooting at the dragon, she was just in the way.

She angled as low as she could, waiting for the tearing pain of a shaft, for the iron grip of talons, for the bite of jaws. A bolt hissed over her shoulder and the dragon screamed behind her. Then she was over the wall, too low, too fast. Corion back-wingedback winged once and they slammed into the ground.

Shouting filled her ears and she was surrounded by armed soldiers. She tried to call her name and group, but her throat was raw from screaming. She coughed, saw someone holding Corion's head. Then a hand reached down and pulled her to her feet.

"Lilka," she gasped. "Fifth regiment scout. News—I have news. About the dragons."

"What news?" A man stepped forward and she saluted when she saw the rank marks on his shoulder.

"Sir. About the dragons. They're controlled by magic. But they only have a short range."

"You'd better tell me more."

\*\*\*

She told the story. Over and over. To this officer, and that officer, and then another officer. Someone brought her a chair and she sank into it gratefully. They questioned her, about Hedersen, about the camp, about what she had seen, about how she had freed the dragon. At one point someone brought in the bone ropes and laid them on the table. She shivered and looked away from the tiny white objects.

Someone woke her before dawn, from a deep sleep. It took

her a moment to realise she was in the ready-room just off the war-room. As she pulled on her boots, she heard the sounds of conversation outside.

She stepped into the war room and paused. A full scout wing, ready for flight, was gathered around the table.

"Here she is." Captain Clarke, the officer who had brought her to the room last evening, beckoned her to join them at the table. She stepped past men and women in flying jackets, grim-faced, but there was something else in the room that had been missing last night.

"Lilka, this is Sergeant Roden. His wing will be doing a sweep across to that town you flew over. If there are any of these circles, we want to destroy them."

"No more dragons?"

"None seen. If we can destroy the circles, we'll be pushing forward tomorrow. Make it clear what they are looking for."

"Sir, I'd like to go too. Then I can show them."

"You don't have to, soldier."

"Yes, sir, I do. If my drake can fly, I'd like permission to go."

Clarke looked at Roden, who smiled at her. "And welcome, scout."

Someone gave her jacket, goggles and gloves, and she pulled on the leather gear as they jogged downstairs. In the dim pre-dawn, the torches on the walls blazed.

Roden handed her a crossbow. "If you see a mage, try to shoot him."

"Scout wings are armed now, sir?"

"Times change, Lilka."

"Yes, sir."

Someone led Corion out, and she checked him over. He was clean, looked tired but bright. He leaned his head down to her and she scratched under his jaw. "No more hiding in the swamp for us," she murmured to him.

Roden gave the signal and they mounted. Lilka turned her face into the wind. It wasn't over. She wondered about the fate of Hedersen and Vander and the soldiers in the internment camp at Jurien. Maybe she would see them again after all.

Roden gave the signal to fly and they launched into the air.

# THE SECOND BATTLE

## Christina Marie

Christina Marie is a college student who prefers daydreaming about fantasy and scifi worlds instead of listening to lectures and writing stories instead of papers. Somehow, she hasn't flunked out. Mostly because half of her classes are in creative writing.

"The Second Battle" came from a creative writing assignment and is Christina's first published piece of fiction. See her blog "Dragons, Zombies, and Aliens" (http://christinamariedza. blogspot.com) for more of Christina's work. Enjoy! :)

The whetstone was an ugly green. Pale, sickly color. But at least it wasn't the color of blood. Jason drew the whetstone across his blade that was well beyond sharp.

Villagers bustled around him. He heard their gentle sobs, their fervent prayers, their angry curses. Out of the corner of his eye he saw the strongest and bravest venture out into the grasslands, bringing back the wounded, identifying the dead. Crows circled the darkening sky. The villagers threw the greenish goblin bodies in a pile and let the birds feast, but chased away any who tried pecking at a human corpse.

Jason didn't offer to help. Didn't comfort those grieving a fresh death. Didn't apply any of his extensive knowledge of warfare to help repair the defenses. He just kept sharpening his blade, keeping his eyes on the perfect reflection of the moon's blinding light.

He wanted to curse his gnarled, calloused hands that shook with arthritis. They'd barely held the sword steady as he'd cut down the goblins and shouted orders. They, and the rest of his aged body, kept him chained to this broken village with its bloody fields and grieving widows.

*Some retirement this is,* he thought.

Jason should have been part of the rescue mission. He should have been leading the team that was tracking the goblins and the villagers they'd kidnapped. He should have been the captain of the second battle.

Thirty years ago, he would have been.

But now, it was his granddaughter, Elise.

He wondered if, right this moment, she was using the sword he'd trained her with. The one he'd made specially for her, even going so far as to add a hawk design to the hilt. Birds had always been her favorite animal. She'd been so happy when he'd given her the sword, her innocent smile lighting up the room.

Gods, Jason's son-in-law had been horrified at the thought of his little girl becoming a soldier like her grandfather. Jason hadn't been too thrilled either (*Look where it's gotten her*). But it wasn't much of a choice out here, where even the safest parts of the country prepared for goblin or orc raids. Elise's father had bitched and bitched, but as he was in the city for business and Elise was in the country with Jason...Well, in any case, Jason doubted that City Boy would have much to complain about now. Those without swords had a better chance of being killed by a sword.

Jason wondered if Elise had found her lover and the other kidnapped villagers, scared and a bit worse for wear, but alive. Or had she only found corpses?

Was she even alive?

Jason gave the sword one last lick of the whetstone, and stared at his blade. An old, tired man stared back, flecks of dried, black goblin blood sprinkled on his face.

Gods, was this what it'd been like for his family all those years ago? This tortured, eternal waiting? Meanwhile, he'd been gallivanting off on adventures in all corners of the world. Battling goblins, waging war on tyrants, outsmarting wizards, even killing a dragon. And he hadn't gotten too hurt with that last one. He'd been too high on pride and stupidity to care about the wounds, anyway. But he knew if Elise ever came home with half as many burns and cuts and broken bones as he had, his old heart would burst. No wonder his mother had been such a fan of whiskey.

When Jason saw his parents, grandparents, and wife in the next world, he was going to throw himself at their feet and beg their forgiveness, for being so carelessly cruel. They had worried themselves into an early grave, and Jason had had the nerve to ask them to wait on him hand and foot between adventures.

*Hm…Elise is going to be exhausted when she returns. She'll need a hot meal and a bath, probably a shoulder to cry on, seeing as she's lost a few friends…*

Jason stood and sheathed his sword.

Enough self-pity. It was time to get to work.

# FLIGHTCRAFT

## Iona Sharma

Iona is a writer, lawyer and
linguaphile, and the product
of more than one country.
Her stories have previously
appeared at Strange Horizons,
Betwixt and GigaNotoSaurus,
among others. She is also
an editor for Luna Station
Quarterly.

She's started to get post through the door now, circulars, letters from the local council, bills, all addressed to Talitha Cawthorne. That was the name she gave the gas board, when she moved in, and the water board, and the name she gave to the lex-engineer who needed it for the new telephone connection, and it was the name on her birth certificate, once.

"Lovely old-fashioned name, Talitha," her landlady said, when she signed the lease. "Arise, little girl, arise? I used to know my divinity, a long time ago. Although I suppose people call you Tali."

"Yes," she said, because that was true, or at least, she remembered being called that, years ago; she wondered if she'd still turn around at the sound of it. "Thank you. Perhaps you can direct me to the nearest grocer's?"

It wasn't far, up on the road towards the airbase. And now this is her third weekly shopping expedition, picking up eggs, bread, Heinz tinned soup, cheese. She leaves the bicycle leaning against a railing—Downham is safe as houses, the estate agent has said—and walks along the road from the little grocer's, past a bookshop with law and lex textbooks in the window, up to a café with a row of tables by the window. There are a couple of other customers: a woman gesturing wildly at the chalkboard menu, and a man moping into a coffee cup the size of a soup bowl. She sips her own drink and looks up at the little biplane rising and circling from the base, diving, looping the loop. She knows the place used to be RAF Downham—it's been in civilian control only a few months—but it seems to have held on to its skilled crafts-people: the plane corners and turns with eerie, tight precision. And perhaps, she's thinking, drinking in a little self-aware-ness with her tea, it's why she's here, after all. She could have gone anywhere, but she's come to a place where they still fly.

The woman at the counter has stopped gesticulating and is now crossing the floor with another soup-bowl coffee cup and a plate of biscuits balanced precariously on a tray. Talitha frowns, looking at all the chairs that she'll have to avoid trip-ping over, gets up and says, "Can I help you with"—and then it's too late.

"Shit!" the woman yells, stumbling against the table. The hot liquid makes a boiling arc above, and Talitha's mind works overtime—Scottish, from the voice; probably demobbed, to be yelling profanity in public places; possibly stationed at the base here in the town?—before she notices the coffee has slopped over the table edge, soaking into her shopping bag. "Oh, I'm so sorry," the woman says, reaching down to pick up the things spilling out across the floor. The liquid has got into the soup tins so the paper wrapping is coming away, the ink on the inside of the labels blurring into feature-less smudges. The metal is visibly tarnishing and the woman groans. "So sorry, I'm going to make your soup go off. Look - what's your name?"

Talitha takes a breath. "Talitha."

"Look, Talitha, give us your napkin, will you?"

Talitha gives it to her. The Scottish woman pulls a soft pencil from her pocket with hands that are covered in inkstains. Working quickly, she sketches a sequence of symbols on the napkin and hands it back to Talitha. "Quick patch," she says.

"When you get home wrap it round the tins with an elastic band, it'll do the trick. I really am sorry. I've lost my assistant at work, everything's at sixes and sevens, it's a wonder I can keep my head screwed on, but that should fix it."

Talitha inspects the napkin, folds it carefully and puts it away in her pocket. "Thank you, ah…"

"Cat. Catriona McDonald." She looks up at the big wall clock and hisses through her teeth. "Shit, shit, I'm late! Nice meeting you. Sorry!"

She flies out of the café, leaping over a cardboard box in the way of the door and disappears in a flash of movement crossing the glass. Surprising herself, Talitha laughs. She finishes her drink, picks up her bags, lets her hand close on the napkin in her pocket, and starts on the walk home.

*** 

Cat thuds into the hangar, slams her coffee down, finger-combs her hair and gets her breath back just in time for the outside door to swing open. She looks up, hoping she's giving the impression of calm competence, and says, "Audrey Knapp?"

"Yes. A pleasure to meet you." Her new client reaches out for a handshake and Cat winces at the amount of ink on her hands. But Mrs Knapp turns over her palms, inspects them with interest and no displeasure, and Cat thinks perhaps she, like Cat herself, considers the stains honourable badges of the trade.

"Catriona McDonald," she says, a little belatedly. "We've corresponded."

"Of course, Miss McDonald." Mrs Knapp smiles at her, but her eyes are on the great structure behind them, the glowing bronzed surfaces of the metal. When she seems to recollect Cat's presence and turns, she's distracted again: this time by the coiled scrolls on Cat's beautiful carved oak desk, the mess of discarded brushes.

"Perhaps you'll call me Catriona," Cat says, smiling. "Or Cat, everyone does."

"Then you must call me Audrey." Mrs Knapp finally drags her gaze back to Cat and smiles back. "Tell me how this is going to work. You said you'd figured out a new method of lexical locomotion—can you explain, please?"

"With pleasure." With sudden decision, Cat walks to the back of the workshop so the whole scene is spread out in front of them. The prototype craft dominates the space in its struts. "You know, of course," Cat says, "that I'm used to working with smaller aircraft. Biplanes, mostly." Almost unconsciously, she looks up to the giant hook in the roof from which they are hung, and the old Moth they're using as a model. "You've seen the wings in the process of the work-ings. I can have craftspeople in here eight hours a day with their brushes, painting the lettering on the outer surfaces. I suppose if there were no need for that, we could use some-thing other than canvas for the wings."

Audrey nods. "But she's going somewhere where canvas won't cut it, I'm afraid."

Not for the first time, Cat wonders what is taking her on this journey—this middle-aged woman of no particular background, deciding suddenly to cross oceans by air and devoting a large portion of her not-inconsiderable resources towards it. Looking at her, Audrey seems to guess what she's thinking. "Peacetime doesn't agree with me," she says, with a studied lightness. "My former husband departed in search of a quiet life." She gives Cat a small, conspiratorial smile. "Now tell me how we're doing this."

"It occurred to me," Cat says, "that you don't have to see the lettering, even on an aircraft—it's just how we happen to do it. Now, if you take the heavy paper"—she points at the burgeoning scrolls on her desk—"and load it safely into the skin of the vessel, for example in the vacuum spaces between the layers of plating, then…"

Audrey smiles. "I understand."

She starts forwards, going to inspect the work, and Cat hangs back to wait for her verdict. Suddenly, a voice pipes up: "How do the letters make it go, then?"

Cat turns to the stranger coming inside from the rain. "Hello?"

"I'm Toby," he chirps—a boy, not quite a young man. "That's m'mum over there. How does it work?"

Cat is thrown off balance for a moment. She considers, then draws a piece of paper towards her. Quickly, she sketches a basic form, and the paper crumples in her hand, becomes a folded swan.

She hands it over to Toby, who accepts it joyfully. "Wow! That's brilliant! How did you do that?"

"It's like mathematics," Cat says. "Once it's written, it can't not be true. See?" She takes the swan back and adds a descending stroke to the character on the neck. It takes flight and flutters around Toby's head.

"Brilliant!" Toby says again. "Do you think I could learn how to do that?"

Cat inclines her head. "Possibly. In earlier days I'd have said you were too old—I started learning when I was twelve." She smiles at the memory. "But the war has turned everything topsy-turvy. If you have the talent, you could be teachable."

Toby is delighted. "Can you show me now?"

Cat grins. "That's not quite how it works. But sit down over there and I'll see what I can do."

He sits down obediently at the empty desk and she gives him

the first exercise from memory. It's no struggle, to remember being twelve years old with a sharp pen in her hand, sketching *open* and *close* and *open* and *close*, making a child's four-fingered fortune teller with the concentration of a chartered craftswoman working on a de Havilland.

"That's kind of you," Audrey says softly, and Cat startles; she hadn't noticed Audrey stepping back from her aircraft. "Sure he's not in anyone's way?"

"He's not," Cat says. The base at Downham is filled with junior craftspeople, but Cat's own assistant and right-hand man left her service only a week earlier to return to civilian life. Cat explained in vain that they were no longer *RAF* Downham; they were civilian lexical engineers working on civilian aircraft. "Not good enough," he said, and departed for a life presumably connecting telephone lines or mass-producing Fords or some such thing. She knows in her heart it's wrong to blame him; she had been feeling it herself in those latter days, the grief and weight of seeing their craft become a part of the government war machine. "I'll need to recruit someone new at some point, I suppose, but right now it's an empty desk."

Audrey nods, her eyes serious. "Right, Miss McDonald," she says. "I've seen what I need to see. I'm impressed with your work. Let me have a quotation for labour and materials and we'll see about getting this thing done."

Cat blinks, surprised. "I thought—I mean"—she pauses, aware she's about to self-sabotage out of nervousness—"that's a very quick appraisal, Mrs Knapp, I had this meeting booked in for the whole afternoon."

"You were head of the engineering corps here, weren't you?" Audrey snaps.

Cat nods, a little unsure of where this is going. "86th Lexical. I had captain's bars, but it's professional courtesy, really. I

never ordered enlisted men about; I did my own job throughout the war."

"You were in charge of this place," Audrey continues, impla-
cable, "and you, and it, are still here. That'll do for me. Toby,
come along."

"Wait!" Toby cries, and waves his little square of paper. It's
half-squashed and covered in inky smudges, but he holds it
quite still in his palm and Cat sees the movement.

"Well done," she says, and looking at his bright, sweet face,
and Audrey's serious one, makes an impulse decision. "Toby,"
she says, "would you like to stay a while?"

***

Talitha is sure it's the right door, with the right voice filtering through it, for five minutes before she brings herself to
turn the handle and go in. Inside, the open hangar space is
familiar, airy under the rafters and filled with light filtering
through dust motes. There is a biplane at the far end—de
Havilland Giant Moth, provides the part of her mind that
never forgets such things: single-engine and four-hundred
mile range—half-occluded by a swarm of craftspeople, sharpening the smudged flying forms and doing something to the
structural lexicography. Something experimental, that same
part of her mind adds, and Talitha turns away sharply.

"Can I help you?" asks a voice, and Talitha looks at the junior
craftswoman with her hands on her hips. "This is a working
hangar, I'm afraid, it's not safe for…"

"Don't be overzealous, Lindy," says a familiar Scottish voice,
and Talitha wheels around. McDonald is there, her arms full
of scrolls of paper. "You're my friend from the café, aren't
you? Let me just—hey, Toby, put these somewhere, will you?"

A boy scurries across from the other side of the hangar and
does so, seemingly delighted to be asked. "So good to see

people happy in their work," McDonald says, sounding quite sincere.

"Your apprentice?" Talitha guesses.

"Not quite." McDonald sits at the edge of a desk—there are a half-dozen of them in a row at this end of the hangar, although only three seem occupied at present. "But the lad has a fancy for the craft, so he's spending a week or two with me to see if it's for him. Lindy, this is—Talitha, isn't it?

Talitha nods.

"This is Lindy, she's helping out on that monster thing over there." The 'monster thing' is the Giant Moth. Lindy nods stiffly and returns to it without another word, striding determinedly across the hangar. "And," McDonald continues, "she's still not quite on board with the whole civilian aspect of our work, these days. I think she misses the barbed wire." She grins. "Anyway, Talitha, what can I do for you? How did the tins hold up?"

"Oh," Talitha says, suddenly brought back to herself. "They were fine, thank you. Ah, you left this in the café the other day, I asked the owner where I might find you, and…"

She trails off awkwardly, but McDonald takes the sketchpad from her. "Thank you!"

She flips through it and Talitha catches sight of a whole multiplicity of forms, some for flying, some for strength, some for precision, some she's never seen before. "Are you in the trade?" she asks, curiously. "Not many laypeople know how valuable one of these things is."

The paper, Talitha knows, has metal filings in the weave—so even a perfectly-executed form will not take, and a craftswoman can practise without accidentally turning her sketchpad into a paper aeroplane. "No," she says. "But I picked up a little bit in the war."

"Right." McDonald nods. "A lot of people did. Well, listen, if you want to come back at twelve, I'll stand you your lunch, all right? It'd have cost me ten times as much to replace this, after all."

Without waiting for agreement, she turns away to her not-quite apprentice and starts giving him a list of forms to memorise; she breaks off in the middle of the last to call some instructions to the team working on the Giant Moth; she breaks off from that to try some new form of her own on her newly-returned sketchpad; then asks the boy to repeat back the first five items on the list. A little bewildered, Talitha goes back into the cool, heavy spring air, and thinks it chilly after the warmth of the space inside.

*\*\**

They have lunch at the same café, though not at the same table. Cat orders toasted sandwiches and tea for them both and goes to fetch them when Mrs Daly behind the counter calls her name. "That the girl who's taken Amelia Pennyroyal's spare room?" she asks Cat. "Odd fish, that. No one knows her here. See if you can find out what brings her to Downham."

"You're a terrible old gossip, Mrs Daly," Cat tells her, and picks up the tray with utmost concentration. She makes it to the table without incident and Talitha looks up and smiles.

"Thank you," she says. "You know, this wasn't necessary."

"Not a bit of it," Cat says, biting into cheese, ham and pickle. "Eat up, it'll get cold. Maybe I should have ordered chips as well. I can, if you want?"

Talitha laughs, surprising herself once again. "I forgot that," she says. "Lex engineers are always hungry. I worked with one chap who had scrambled eggs on the hour. It was quite endearing."

"I've read theories that say it's some of our energy that makes things fly," Cat says, composedly. "Even if it's not, it's thirsty work. Where were you stationed?"

The sudden shift in conversation startles Talitha. "A long way from here," she says, after a moment. "Up north. You know," she adds, "there's money in wires and cables, these days. Telegraphic lex engineers, household appliances, that sort of thing."

Cat nods. "And there always will be. When I'm old and not on the top of my game any more, that's what I'll do." She has a craftswoman's dispassionate assessment of her own skills, Talitha notices. "But right now—Toby, wee Toby, you met him. Well, his mother has an idea for a new kind of plane. Further, faster, with proper long-range cargo. It's all to do with a stronger physical skin, maybe made out of metal. When I can't fly any more, that's when I'll do household appliances."

Talitha nods in return. "Metal, though? Won't that stop the forms from executing?"

"Somewhat," Cat says, "but it's not an absolute effect, it depends on other factors and I'm hoping we can work around it. I'll show you the diagrams if you like."

"Miss McDonald…"

"Cat."

"Cat," Talitha says. "Should you be telling me this? If it's a private commission, and…"

Cat sighs. "You sound just like Lindy," she says. "Listen, Talitha. I was born into the trade. I got my charter mark when I was twenty."

Talitha whistles involuntarily—she knew, of course, that Cat's talent was something out of the ordinary—but perhaps hadn't quite grasped the extent of it. She says nothing.

"And during the war," Cat continues, "I had to do some

things I wasn't proud of. I built new, improved lightweight planes that dropped new improved heavy artillery, and I put planes back together faster than the medics could put together the pilots. And I did it all behind the barbed wire up there." She motions to the window and the road up to the base. "No apprentices and not accountable to anyone, though my charter swears I'll teach my craft to anyone who asks. They can do proprietorial washing machines, frankly, I don't give a damn. But anyone who wants to fly gets to learn how."

Cat knows when she's finished speaking that she must be flushed with emotion—it's a practised spiel that nevertheless works its way through her body every time, like a form through canvas. But she looks up and Talitha is smiling at her, tentative, luminous. "I understand that," she says.

"We could do this again," Cat says, suddenly. "I mean, it's nice to have company at lunchtimes. It's been lonely since everyone up at the base started to leave."

"I'd like that," Talitha says, and she's smiling again.

*** 

"What happens," Toby asks, "If I do this?"

He picks up his pen—privately, Cat notes his grip has got much better: firm between forefingers and thumb—and rests the nib on his own wrist. He glances up at Cat, then stubbornly begins to sketch a form, a simple one for flight that's on the list that she drills him on every day. He reaches the end, smudges the ink and then looks disappointed. "Oh."

Cat breathes in and shoves down her immediate reaction, which is to grab the pen from his hand. "What were you hoping for?" she asks, keeping her voice gentle. "That you could sketch out *avis-alpha-b* and up, up and away!"

"Alpha-b?" he asks, distracted, and she shakes her head.

"A little beyond your pay grade, I think. You

need to get *avis-unmarked* absolutely spot-on before we do the variations. And soon I'll have to think about getting the first-year syllabus for you. I'll make a note."

"Cat," he says, a hint of a whine coming into his voice. "Tell me."

She relents after a moment, putting a hand on his shoulder. "Toby, you mustn't try and do forms on yourself like that. Not on yourself or anyone else. Do you understand?"

"Why not?" He looks up at her in confusion, and Cat reminds herself that he isn't like she was; he wasn't born into this life.

"There are long textbooks about it," she says, after a moment, "which you'll have to read before you get your charter mark." His eyes shine at that and Cat realises that it's because she's talking about his charter mark, as though it's a given that he will get it, some day. "But for now: think about it like robbing Peter to pay Paul. You can't burn up the energy in your own body that way. What's the First Axiom of the craft of flight?"

In his frustrated expression, Cat sees herself at his age, and smiles beatifically. Finally, he says: "Remember Icarus."

Cat nods. "That's right. Don't do that, Toby. It doesn't work, and it's not" - she hesitates - "it's not right. Promise me you won't do that again."

Toby glances up at her. "I promise."

"There's a good boy." She ruffles his hair and he ducks away, heading across the hangar presumably in an attempt to escape both form drills and gestures of affection.

"That's not quite it, you know," Talitha says, emerging from the shadows behind the prototype. The aircraft is about half-done and is beginning to take on a personality of her own. Cat can't quite see the shape of her yet, except in shadows and absence, like a dry patch under a tree in the rain. It'll come.

"What's that?" she asks, as Talitha walks out from under a wing.

"What you said to Toby." Talitha looks at her, her eyes dreamy. "It's not quite right. There are some forms which will work on skin. If someone else draws them."

"Oh," Cat says. Before she can think of anything to say, Talitha is gone, edging back into the dimness behind the aircraft, heading for the door out to the sky.

***

Cat formally declares Toby her apprentice after he's been hanging around the hangar for a month. "Getting in the way," Lindy says, but Cat knows that's not right. The lad has fetched and carried messages, stirred great pots of ink, trimmed brushes, got up early and stayed late. Cat herself was born into pre-war privilege, the daughter and granddaughter of flight craftswomen; she respects the boy scrabbling for his start.

Audrey is grim but accepting, when she visits next. "God knows it's in his blood," she says. "His father was a crafts-man. A mediocre one, mind you, never stretched to anything but rivets and joins. But it's a trade for the boy."

Cat smiles, then feels herself grow abruptly serious. "I'll do my best by him," she promises, "but my best isn't what it might have been. Before the war I'd have sent him to Woolwich for his theory, and he could have come here for his practical, but since the war..."

Audrey holds up a hand. "I'm grateful for whatever you can give him, Miss McDonald."

"Call me Cat," Cat says, for at least the fiftieth time, and smiles again. "Would you like to see how the work is progressing?"

"I would, thank you," Audrey says, and this time, as Cat shows her around the bare skeleton of the aircraft, she's less nervous: she knows the work is good. She and her people have been scratching forms and grammar on scraps of paper, making tiny models to dart around the hangar; they've been testing materials out on the hill, in the full blast of the wind; they've been consulting the sort of textbooks the craftspeople often leave for the academics. The aircraft doesn't yet look very different from any other of its size - the forms have been done on the usual heavy paper and then laid on the surface of the metal plating; Cat means to have them put within the skin only when everything is complete - but she's aware on a subconscious level that this one is different. A different presence, she thinks to herself, then smiles at her own fancy.

"It looks like you're making good progress," Audrey says, with reserve; Cat thinks that she probably doesn't say anything she doesn't mean, and keeps on smiling. "Have you considered a name, yet?"

"For the type?" Cat shakes her head. "Not yet. We might have to move away from the" - she gestures at the Giant Moth they were using as a model, now on the other side of the hangar from the prototype - "insect theme."

"For the particular craft." Audrey is hesitant. Nervous, Cat realises. "I don't know what the custom is, with these things - for the builders of the craft to name her, or for..."

"Oh," Cat says, and then, gently, "I think you should name her. If she's your" - Cat pauses - "unquiet life."

Audrey gives her a half-smile. "In that case," she says, "I suppose I'll have to think of something."

And after that, Cat thinks she's forgotten - after another week, some of the metal plating is appearing, and craftswomen in the hangar are calling it the Beast and the Thing and other such hefty monosyllables, so Cat thinks she's not the only one to have felt the presence of it, sitting squat in the hangar - but then Audrey asks, in a routine letter that otherwise deals with quotations for further materials, how they're getting on with *Margaretha Zelle*.

"Mata Hari!" Talitha says, startled, when Cat tells her.

"I had to look it up," Cat says, ruefully, over a cheese bloomer. "I don't know much about - well, anything that's not flightcraft."

"That's understandable," Talitha says. She seems amused, taking a bite into her own sandwich with piccalilli. It's a bright, breezy day, so they're sitting on the hill on the grass and holding on tightly to the sandwich wrappers. "I don't suppose you've ever had much time for anything else."

"And you should forgive me if I'm wrong," Cat says, tentatively, "but wasn't she a spy for the other side?"

"Brave as anything, though," Talitha says, and Cat is content to take her word for it.

*** 

Not long after that, Cat needs a favour.

"You're afraid of flying!" Talitha says, and chuckles. A shared and excellent steak pie has just rather robbed them of any great urgency to return to work.

"Not at all," Cat says, primly. "It was part of my training. But"—she pauses—"Miller, my old assistant, you know. He used to do it. When they wanted a craftsperson along on a test flight."

"Seems to me they ought to have one along on every test flight," Talitha says. "I'll do it, Cat. But you should try it sometime."

"Oh, no," Cat says, "no" - and then almost gets knocked flying onto the grass. "Lindy!" she says, stepping backwards. "Don't rush about so! What is it?"

"You've got to come," Lindy says, breathless and incoherent, "I called the fire brigade but they won't come in time, you've got to, Cat…"

She turns and runs back up the hill, her wildly scrabbling feet pushing up tufts. Cat follows her up and into the hangar, pushing open the little door with her eyes on her feet, so it takes her another second to look up and swear extravagantly. *Margaretha Zelle* had been hung from the roof: now she's half on the floor, great strips of paper hanging from the now-bent hook, and one of her wings is almost broken off, turned into a shapeless mess from the impact. "Is there someone under there? When did it happen?"

"Toby," Lindy says, tearful but steady, "he was looking at the forms, he was trying to figure out the pattern. Just a minute ago, Cat, he wasn't under the fuselage, he was under the wing, he might be…"

"Shut up, all of you," Cat snaps out, with military sharpness. "Not a word! Now."

In that textured silence, the paper flaps in the draught, a drop of water falls from the roof, and from the left wing of the stricken aircraft, two metres down and along, something - someone - taps. "Toby?" Cat says, loud and clear. "Tap twice if that's you."

Tap, tap.

"Tap if it's just you under there."

Tap.

"And once more if you're hurt."

Tap.

"All right," Cat says, clapping her hands. "The fire brigade have to come all the way from King's Lynn, we can't wait for them."

"Cat," Talitha says, urgently, "the plane's on the edge." She gestures at the hook, at where part of the structure remains suspended. "If we pull or tug at it, we might bring the whole thing down. It might crush..."

"Understood." Cat breathes. "We need to lift it. Not manually, you know how. None of you distract me for the next two minutes." She's getting down on her knees as she speaks, drawing forms quickly on the sheets laid out on the hangar floor. It's only the skill of long, long practice that keeps them neat and true. She draws strokes in abbreviated forms, crossing out rather than erasing her mistakes, waiting for them to execute; she thinks for a second about the hook she hadn't even considered, designed to hold up aircraft made out of canvas and not metal, then pushes away the thought. It's not useful.

"Cat," Talitha says, gently, "I can help"—and Cat wants to cry over the junior craftsmen who departed for telephone engineering, rather than do this work that matters.

"Do the groundwork," she tells Talitha, screwing pieces of paper into tiny balls and throwing them north, northwest, north-northwest. Talitha follows them and lays down the right forms for rigidity and tension, not with textbook perfection, but with the fluid essentials.

"You'll put yourself into a coma if you try this with no help," she says, without looking up. "There's not enough push in the forms for you to lift this alone."

Cat gestures wildly and put in a cross-stroke. "No other option."

Talitha holds up her pen and pulls up her sleeves, exposing the unmarked skin of her forearms.

"You're mad," Cat breathes.

"It's energy," Talitha says, with head back down. "It will fuel"—she draws a form in the air, and Cat breathes in sharply—"under the wing, if you—look, Cat, we don't have time to argue over this. Say yes or wait for the fire brigade."

Cat stares at her for another moment, then pulls up her own sleeves. "I didn't mean *you*," Talitha snaps, a little panicky, then begins to draw. Cat's fingertips are on the edge of the sheet and as the forms take shape something crackles at the paper's edge. Cat stares at it in bemusement, not thinking about the pain, as the fire catches and carries along the sheet and in its wake Talitha sketches out form after form, ones Cat only knows from textbooks, with no time to perfect her work before it's sacrificed to the flames.

"Done," Talitha says, and the two of them look at each other, then both reach downwards. Cat has time for fear, feeling her eyebrows singe and the roaring heat inches from her bare hands—and then they press the new sheet of paper down onto the aircraft wreckage, the flames leaping across. They only have a minute or two, Cat thinks, before the metal starts to heat up.

"Now!" Talitha yells, and Cat adds one more form with a hand that barely grips, simple enough for an apprentice to have done it—*avis-unmarked*, a stylized bird, for flight—and the broken pieces explode upwards.

Before Cat can move, Talitha dives in, grabs Toby, covered in dust, with blood showing at his mouth, then goes back to check there's no one else there. "Go!"

"Get back!" Cat presses both hands down, bloody and ruinous, destroying all the forms. The mess of the wing rattles down like unholy rain, Cat's knees hit the ground and the last thing she remembers is the sound of steam hissing, and Talitha's voice, soft and determined, as she calls to the others, as she pours water on the flames.

***

"Mrs Knapp," Cat's saying, not for the first time, "I'm so, so sorry" - and Audrey stamps her foot.

"Cat, with all due respect, shut up," she says. "It's a fat lip and a broken leg. Toby's had worse playing cricket. And even if he hadn't, it wouldn't have been your fault."

"He's my apprentice," Cat says, stubborn and frustrated, "he's my apprentice, and I should have protected him, and I should have..."

"Cat," Audrey interrupts, "if you must make a martyr of yourself, go back to fixing my aeroplane. I will take Toby home for a while and run him back to you when he's ready. A very good day to you both."

She bows, turns on her heel and stalks out of the hangar. In the ensuing dusty silence, Talitha sighs. "She's right," she says, tentatively; Cat has not been easy to talk to, these last few days. "It's not your fault."

She waves vaguely as she says it: *Margaretha Zelle* is still spread in pieces across the hangar floor, though the remaining craftspeople have been working hard to remove the destroyed pieces, as not to warp the whole. Before Cat can say anything else, Talitha adds, "How's Lindy?"

"She says she's feeling a little better," Cat says, sounding defeated. Other than Talitha herself, Lindy had the worst of the smoke inhalation and falling debris. "She's going to stay with her sister-in-law for a few days."

"Glad to hear it," Talitha says, and then stops short. "The first part, I mean. And - Cat. What about you?"

"What about me?"

"How are you?" Talitha asks, insistent. "Cat, you lifted that wing more or less entirely by yourself. I know I helped make the thing susceptible, but you made it fly." She pauses. "I've seen what happens when people do mad things like that."

"Mad things like that," Cat repeats, with something in her expression that Talitha can't read. After a moment Cat gets to her feet, slowly and stiffly—Talitha wasn't wrong that what she did has taken the energy out of her - and beckons imperiously. "Come with me, please."

Curious, Talitha follows. Outside the hangar, on the grassy hillside, Cat sits down on a soft tussock and leans backwards, looking right up at the sky. She doesn't speak for a couple of minutes, and Talitha reaches over and touches her shoulder. "Cat?"

Still silence. Cat takes a number of deep, steady breaths. Talitha is starting to wonder if she's ever going to speak when Cat finally sighs and says, "So. These forms." She pulls back her sleeves as she says it, showing the damage: the lexical cuts are healing faster than the burns around them.

Talitha looks across at her face. "Yes. What about them?"

"I'm not sure," Cat says, mild. "I've been wondering, you see, if you might have used them in the war. If that's how you know what you know."

"You've worked it out, then," Talitha says, dispassionately.

"Have I?" Cat says, still looking straight up. "I don't know what I've worked out. I do know the old stories, about people who work with skin, and blood, and all those things that are neither ink nor paper."

"Mostly," Talitha says, sighing, "I worked with ink and paper. Mostly, but not always."

"Can you tell me?"

"I probably shouldn't." Talitha shrugs. "It was a place up north, somewhere near Loch Laggan, if you know it. If an aircraft came down with something interesting in the visible lexicography, that's where the pieces were brought. And..." - she pauses, then goes on - "with them, they brought the pilots."

"I was approached, myself," Cat says, matter-of-fact. "Just a few weeks after the declaration, actually. Someone came up to me in a café in Soho and said they'd known my father. They probably did, at that. Told me about the importance of the war effort. And how everything could be a weapon in the wrong hands. Asked me to consider a role in *special operations*, italicised, and awaited my answer."

Talitha shakes her head in return, impatient. "You said no."

"I want to say I thought about it," Cat says. "I want to say I had that kind of... courage? But I sent him away and he didn't come back. Tell me, what forms did you use on the pilots?"

"Lapidary forms, with proprietary modification." Talitha shrugs again and gestures. "If you work them on rock, it crumbles."

"Jesus Christ." Cat puts both her hands over her eyes, and Talitha flinches.

"We didn't all have the luxury of the long way around," she says, more sharply than she'd meant; she does not care about Cat's opinion of her, not about this. "We didn't all have the kind word, the fair start. We weren't all like Toby, or..."

"Me." Cat hasn't moved. "All of us raised in the grand old tradition. Remember Icarus. Help all who ask for it. Thou shalt not kill. Did you..."

"Yes. When it could not possibly be avoided."

"For information?"

"Among other reasons." She pauses. "You saw the value of generating energy in a hurry."

Cat looks up at her, something awful in her eyes. "Christ."

"Cat." Talitha stands up and takes a step downhill. "I did what I did. And I saved Toby's life. Yours, too, in the war. A dozen times, perhaps, without your knowing it. If you call it dirty work, well, I'm not here to answer to you."

She's trembling a little as she walks down the hill, but not too much. She's thinking about the pretty little room she's renting from an old lady who's kind to her, and how she came here where they still fly.

"Talitha." Cat scrambles to her feet, swaying slightly. "Stop, please."

Talitha says, over her shoulder, "Perhaps you should have waited till the fire brigade came from Lynn. Perhaps you should have let the undercarriage tip and crush Toby's bones."

Cat makes a frustrated noise and holds up her palms, still partly bandaged, all the exposed flesh shiny and raw. "Talitha…"

"Your own skin was in the form you made," Talitha says, and she'd meant to walk away, but she's turned on the spot, facing up. "Burnt away. Don't talk to me about clean hands."

"I'm not, for God's sake," Cat says, staggers and lands on the grass, makes a muted noise of pain, and moves no further. Talitha takes one more step, and has a sudden memory of meeting Cat in the village cafe, the rising arc of boiling coffee, the tins of tomato soup that are still sitting on her shelf at home, now sealed for all time, or at least until she stops having lunch with Cat every day. With a groan, she starts back upwards.

"You did your own war work, Cat," she says, half with anger and half something else, as she gives Cat a hand to steady herself with, and sits back down beside her. "You told me yourself."

Cat just looks at her. "I know."

"And," Talitha says, cuttingly, "you implemented what I

learned. What I got from them, and the improvements you made..."

"I know."

"You might not have done the work, but you..."

"I know!" Cat puts her head in her hands, then looks up. "For goodness' sake, Talitha. I know what I did."

"Well, then," Talitha says, hands shaking.

For a moment, there's only silence. Then Cat leans back and breathes out, and her expression slowly loses some of that bleakness. "Believe it or not, Talitha, before the accident I was planning to offer you a job."

Talitha stares. "What?"

Cat nods. "Lindy and the juniors are good and sweet and Toby has promise, but I need a real second."

Talitha's still staring. "You want me to be your assistant?" She pauses. "I mean—you still do?"

"My right hand." Cat gestures with her actual right hand, the bandages making the point. "Will you consider it?"

"I don't have your qualifications."

"We'll put you in for your exams when Toby does his. Will you do it?"

Talitha says, "Even if I do, I won't apologise for who I am, Cat. Nor what I did. I don't need your forgiveness."

"I used to build efficient aircraft," Cat says, softly and sadly, "delivering efficient artillery, on top of people. I don't know what happens, about that." She spreads her palms. "I told you before, I don't know much that isn't flightcraft. I don't know about what's written, what's true. Thou shalt not kill and all that. But I've got to rebuild that damn aircraft, Audrey's bought her goggles. I've got to get the new syllabus for Toby, and I need to send a get-well card to Lindy and I need to put in an order for a few hundredweight of wing canvas and I need to not be sat on my arse on a damp hillside, and I need your help."

Talitha grins, suddenly. "All right," she says. "On one condition." She holds out a hand to Cat, who takes it, and between them they get Cat to her feet. "When she's built, you'll fly in her."

"Oh, no, no," Cat says. "Don't even think about it."

Talitha shakes her head. Despite the chaos in the hangar, out here in the wind and the sun, she can imagine *Margaretha Zelle* clearly, how strange and beautiful she'll look, with forms hidden within her skin and so much more than she seems. "Don't worry," she says, giving Cat a shoulder to lean on, "I'll teach you how."

"All right," Cat says, sounding entirely defeated, "if that's what it takes"—and Talitha laughs as they go on up the hillside, into the curve of the sky.

# PRELUDE

## Sian M. Jones

Sian M. Jones received an MFA
from Mills College in 2004.
Her work has appeared in Best
New American Voices 2006,
The Montucky Review, and The
Cheat River Review.

Pre kept her Familiar™ hidden under her jacket, because she knew the sight of it unnerved people. The tiny metal figure, the size and shape of a chameleon, clinging to her collar or her sleeve. It was more than out-of-fashion—it upset people, this visible evidence of her deviation from the norm.

Her nearest flat-neighbor, Subomi, at least kept a sense of humor about it. "I can't believe you're holding out! The Implants, they're so—intuitive." She'd opened her hand then, palm up, spread the fingers, and the light flickered above her palm, the hologram emitted by her own flesh, a three-dimensional light sculpture. And the way the data hummed through your own nerves, Subomi described it as warm, thrilling. A summer breeze inside the body.

"Qua and I get along just fine," Pre had said. The little robot had been curled up near her collarbone, a weight as familiar as a piece of jewelry, brilliant silver against her dark-brown skin.

But she'd been on the Transport enough times, on her way to work, and seen the looks in other people's eyes. Well, if they were looking. Most of the time, they were focused on the hol-oregisters in their own hands, or staring at a stream of data across their retinas. But sometimes their eyes would focus, they'd blink, snapped out of that trance, out of that singular oneness of themselves and the data, and they'd see her staring there, with her Familiar, separate.

"It's so—archaic!" said Subomi, still with that open wonder in her voice.

Yes. There was something archaic about it. She wasn't unified with Qua. She had to work to communicate with it. She observed and Qua observed the same events, separately, and sometimes came up with different observations. Most of the time, the robot anticipated her needs, her responses. Reached out its small, three-toed claw and touched her bare skin. There would be that brief shock, the static electricity, and then the presence in her mind of what the robot had seen, images from a slightly different angle, and even stranger—interpretations, listed in an orderly fashion, World Data searches for relevant terms, the names of texts, the faces of people who might answer questions. When they saw a man playing a violetric at the Transport platform, she saw a man she didn't know. Qua gave her his name, pulled from facial recognition against police records: he was a drifter, a thief, with several arrests for vagrancy. But the music he was playing was so beautiful—what was it? Qua answered, Composition *343, composed by Wellis Ọgụgụọmakwa, 20 years ago, debuted at the Abuja Opera House in the spring, on a Sunday night. It rained throughout the concert. Pre thought for a moment that she could hear the rain, and whether the sound was part of the music itself or whether it was the actual soundtrack of the actual rainstorm taken from some weather observational tower tucked amidst the minarets of that massive city where the music had first been played, she didn't know. And she liked not knowing. She liked that moment when it was just her in her thoughts, in her head. And she liked the moment when Qua entered her thoughts, with its little electric sizzle. She liked that it felt like a conversation more than a data delivery. She liked that it seemed to be flavored by Qua, but she herself ultimately made the choice about what details to distinguish, what searches to pursue, what images to linger over.

She didn't think that people with the Implants were given that chance, that split second. That free will.

But she couldn't say that to Subomi, because Subomi was so happy, so unconcerned; she even seemed rewarded by being part of some instantaneous, never-ending hive mind. To be honest, Pre wasn't surprised at her own silence—there was a lot she couldn't say to Subomi. I love you, she couldn't say. I want you—she couldn't say. Even as she looked at Subomi, at the freckles over her high cheeks, at the caramel-colored skin along her throat, at the way her hennaed dreadlocks gathered and swung as she gestured enthusiastically. When they met in the Court, that common area in the enormous block of flats they both lived in, and Subomi sat with her, telling her about her day, asking her questions about hers, all Pre could do was think: Be quiet, shhh, so quiet. Don't interrupt the flow of Subomi's words. Don't give her a reason to stop.

It was more complicated than a lack of confidence on Pre's part. The problem was that Pre paid too much attention to the type of person Subomi showed desire for, and she knew that wasn't her. When she was younger she might have tried to change it—might have grown her hair out or put on head-dresses or enormous skirts or layers of sheath-dresses. But by now, in her late 20s, Pre was who she was: unadorned by any piercings or tattoos, her hair shaved in close black spirals on her scalp, her clothes plain and unelaborate. She'd settled into drone clothes and easy care and the little natural beauty she thought she had.

So, at the end of their conversations in the Court, Subomi would go back to her flat, and Pre would go back to her flat, those boxes meant only for sleep, and they would never invite one another in.

If she had invited Subomi in, she would have seen on the

dresser the evidence, the secret reason Pre kept Qua. Two small robots, defunct. Not sleeping, but dead. They'd died the day her parents had. What data they had in them was locked away behind bioencoding; only her parents' own living bodies could have unencrypted them, opened them up. Even so, she'd carried their little metal corpses from place to place since the day of their deaths. Each place she'd slept in, she'd made a corner into a shrine where she'd lay the robots next to each other, draping their limp, articulated limbs one over the other—into an embrace. Each night, this was where she laid Qua, next to the Familiars of her parents. She would hold the little robot in her hands, make a child's wish over it, and set it down beside them. The little robot would circle the couple, chirruping, its scales rising and then falling together with a gentle clink. The robot would curl up beside one or the other of the couple, and relax into sleep mode, motionless.

It was a ridiculous wish. That one day Qua would unlock the barriers between it and the other robots. It would be able to access their memory, stored in the super-efficient crystals at the heart of each mechanical body, and it would share that memory with her. She would see her parents again—or at least see through their eyes. She would hear them. She would smell them. They would be in her head as concretely as the data was.

The real memories were stored inside her own brain, of course, and that was the failure. Those memories degraded. Each time she pulled them up from synaptic storage, she'd rewrite them somehow, without meaning to. The memory became about the emotion of now, no longer the emotion of then, and the details—sounds, smells, confirmations, contra-dictions— were missing, overlapping, smeared. A palimpsest. Unreadable.

The last time her parents had been alive, the last time she'd been with them, she'd been too young to have a Familiar. It wasn't until she was twelve that her aunt got her Qua. From that point on, the robot could corroborate her own memories. But before that point, all she had was memory corruption.

So, despite the ridiculousness, despite knowing it was magical thinking, she would think hard and heartfelt at Qua when they were communing just before bed: Find a way in. Find them.

And the little robot would reply, a soft trill in Pre's mind: Searching...

There were also those mornings when she would wake up, and Qua would be curled up on the pillow next to her head. Yes, she'd put it on the dresser before bed. Yes, she'd seen it shut down to rest. But still she would open her eyes, and there it would be, beside her face, in sleep mode. It seemed to know when she opened her eyes. Probably the shift in her body's electrical field told it when she was no longer fully asleep, but it always delighted her—how as soon as she opened her eyes, it would open its own bright-bulb eyes and lift its tiny articulated head and emit a whir.

It seemed to say: Good morning.

If she waited too long, it would reach out a three-toed claw to her nose, to her cheek, and zap her. Connect. Fill her head with data all at once. The importance, the urgency of data. Propulsion. And Pre would reach up and remove the claw. "Too early," she'd say. "Knock it off." She'd close her eyes for a few minutes more—until she felt the tiny sharp of a single connection point, as if to say: Now. Why not now? Now. Why not now?

Of course she'd eventually give in. She'd sit up and let the robot climb up the length of her sleeping shift's sleeve to perch on her shoulder. And she'd start the day.

At first, Pre had wondered if there was a malfunction in the robot's battery. Was it running out of power at some time in the night and coming to her for what little kinetic energy it could pick up from her sleeping body? But she'd taken Qua in for service then—as difficult as it was to find technician, she knew of one, by word-of-mouth among other Familiar-users—and the technician had given its power system the all-clear.

Pre was left with the conclusion that the robot was making a choice to sleep beside her—though even the Familiars' own engineers would not have said that the robot made per-sonal choices, not in the information it presented, or in the moment it chose to present them. It was merely mathematical calculation, that split second between the observation and connection, and a host of algorithms finely-calibrated to Pre's own mind. The engineers would argue that the robot was reading Pre's own anxieties about lateness or laziness when it made her get up. She couldn't help thinking that her own enjoyment of lying there should have been the overwhelm-ing need that the robot might have picked up on, but then she knew that she was such a maelstrom of needs and fears and strong unconscious wishes that it was possible she herself misperceived what was the dominant, the ultimately more important. Maybe it was just that, given that minute separa-tion, the distance between Pre's skin and the Familiar's metal shell, that observer's standpoint, the robot knew her better than she knew herself.

She must be pretty far gone in her loneliness, she thought, to attribute agency, let alone wisdom, to a device.

\*\*\*

Pre had some warning of larger developments when her work superior called her to his end of the shared workspace. The echo-room seemed particularly brightly-lit and exposed that morning. She'd walked down the length of the slim work surface to him, past the line of her data-entranced colleagues, their Implants playing white noise or music into their ears to give them aural privacy, their eyes fixed on the thin, translucent screens in front of them. Their Implants logged them directly into the corporate data stream.

The new superior—what was his name? She couldn't even be bothered. He looked up from his screen when she finally reached him and said, "Ekwensi. We need to talk about your data interface."

She'd blinked at him, felt Qua shift slightly, its scales lifting just a little. Could her superior hear that small whir, like a question? Or was it just her?

"Sir?"

"Your technology is obsolete. Statistics show that worker efficiency increases 27% with the Implants. Twenty-seven is not a small number, Ekwensi."

"No, sir. It isn't." This superior was new, younger than the last one. He wore his management position like a newly-ironed shirt, preening stiffly so as not to wrinkle it. She reached for the explanation that usually seemed to calm such concerns. "I can't afford the Implants right now."

What would she say when the company finally decided to pay for its employees' Implants? How would she fend that off? Mostly, she relied on the company's never reaching that point—the board would never put aside their immediate greed for some uncertain future return. Better to make the workers pay for their own means to work.

Her superior was looking at her more directly than usual. "Ekwensi, I don't think you can afford not to."

"I'm sorry?" Familiars didn't, couldn't breathe, but Qua's little scales raised and lowered themselves like gills. Pre felt the flutter of it inside her collar.

"You understand what I'm saying." He let those words rest there a moment. Then, as he was turning back to his screen, he said, "This job requires new technology. You're falling behind your colleagues."

Well, of course he turned away from her on that statement. It was a blatant lie. Her numbers were still the highest in the section. It's true that sometimes she wandered off in her investigations, and her analyses encompassed more complex factors, subtle contributions, tributaries of effect. , Where where the analyses of her colleagues were so shallow, so rote. How often had she wondered whether their search hypotheses guided their results? How often did they stop to consider their observational bias? Did they ever do more than the minimum scrutiny of either the research premises or the patterns in the data they thought they perceived?

She could raise her voice. She should raise her voice.

She felt the pinprick of one of Qua's toes, right in the softness of her neck. A spark and then that voice inside her head (it always sounded like a version of her own voice, of course): Calm. This is unimportant.

If any device other than Qua had tried to give her that message, she would have bucked against it. But Qua added soothing images, a beach she'd visited with her parents when she was a child, choosing shells from the sand, rinsing them in the waves. The waves, clear, distilled, cleaned by the Transport-sized filters at the mouth of the bay. The water was cool, but not cold. It washed in and out. In and out.

She supposed that when they did force her to get the Implants, there would be scenes like this in her head all day long. She would never not need soothing. Of course, the Implants could adjust her hormone levels directly, dialing down the adrenaline, wafting gently higher the endorphins, until she was nothing but a bird in flight—lazy, contented flight. She wouldn't even know that she was being soothed. Even before she was angry, she would be defused.

How would she know herself, under such conditions? And how long would knowing herself even matter?

You will outlast him. A shiver against her neck.

She smiled to herself. Yes, she'd outlasted other superiors. One more wouldn't be too much effort.

*** 

That night, Pre was sitting in the Court with Subomi when Qua communicated the appointment. They had been mid-conversation when the robot, who had been sitting quietly on Pre's thigh, reached over and touched her wrist.

Subomi noticed the pause while the message was communicated, and smiled as she waited. When Pre's focus came back to her, she said, "What is it?"

"A reminder for a physician's appointment tomorrow."

"Ah, that's sounds helpful, then. Are you feeling alright? I didn't know you were going to the doctor."

"Neither," said Pre, "did I."

Subomi laughed. "What do you mean?"

"I didn't make an appointment."

"Are you sure? Maybe you made it and forgot?"

Pre ran a finger down the length of Qua's back. It was smooth, mostly, except for the minute ridges at the edge of each line of scales. Tiny, microscopic bumps, really. Slight raised lines. Braille.

Really? She she thought at the robot.

The robot hummed assent.

She should have seen the larger pattern—the conversation at work, and now this appointment made without her knowledge, on her behalf—but at the time, she simply found herself thinking: Did you make this appointment for me,

Qua? Do you think I'm getting sick? What need are you anticipating now?

There was no answer to a question like that. Qua buzzed patiently in her brain, waiting until she phrased its search parameters in language it could understand.

So she went back, complacently, to the satisfaction of chatting with Subomi.

*** 

When Pre signed in at the physician's office, the receptionist didn't even bother to look up from the holograms on her open palms.

"I'm sorry," said Pre, not sorry at all for interrupting. "But could you tell me what reason was given for this appointment?"

"One moment, please. I'm accessing that data." The woman's eyes flitted back and forth, her head not moving. It was odd, thought Pre, how much it seemed like the rapid eye movement of sleep, more than the natural motion of an eye reading data. "It looks like you've already had your preliminary assessment. Congratulations, Mx. Prelude Ekwensi, you have been approved for implantation today."

Pre went very still, then, and if she didn't know better, she'd say Qua, nestled in the crook of her arm, under her loose sleeve, went a few degrees colder. "I'm sorry, what?"

"We no longer require fasting on the day of implantation, and all your blood results indicate compatibility, so, yes, I don't see any obstacles to going forward today."

Pre felt her body reacting. She felt the rush of blood into her limbs, she felt the release of adrenaline, which felt like fear. "I didn't make this appointment," she said.

"Ah," said the receptionist, her eyes still on the data. "Yes, we've been seeing this a lot with the old Familiar users. It's a glitch. The appointments don't get logged by the diary function, but they do get logged by the calendar function, and so the appointment reminder comes as a bit of a surprise." The woman bared her official smile at Pre, but still didn't look at her.

"I'm telling you, I didn't make this appointment. I wouldn't have made this appointment."

The woman nodded as if in sympathy. "I am sorry that the engineers haven't isolated the problem with the Familiars' code on this matter, but it'll all be moot, won't it? After today. You'll have your glitch-free Implants."

What white noise, what corporate doublespeak was playing in this woman's ears that she didn't hear, couldn't hear what Pre was saying? Pre leaned close to the receptionist, trying to get into her line of vision. "I did not make this appointment. I do not want implantation. I need you to put in a stop-order now."

"I don't understand, Mx. Ekwensi. I show all the authorizations have been acquired. Your psychological evaluation indicated a particular eagerness to transition to the new technology. If other factors have arisen since your assessment, you can inform the doctor and —"

Pre slapped her hands against the woman's desk. "Gods, woman, I never had that assessment. You don't even know that the Implants are compatible with my biology. You might be killing me. Do you understand? I could have a fatal reaction. I could die!"

Even now the woman wouldn't look at her. Her official smile had dropped from her face, and Pre could see her racing through the data, the holograms flickering on and on and on.

"You'll need to discuss this with the physician, Mx. Ekwensi."

No, Pre knew. No. Things would proceed as scheduled once

she was inside the office. An anxiolytic would be administered—if not outright sedation. She would be trying to mumble her objections through lips that could not move.

It was then she noticed the silence. Qua wasn't communicating with her. As far as she could tell, the robot was still attached to the inside of her sleeve. It was curled up like a large pill bug, a round bead that swayed when she moved. But no communication, no contact. No data outside of her own mind.

It should have panicked her. Instead, it made her calm.

Above all, she advised herself, seem cooperative. "All right," she said. She gave her best show of false contentment, arranging the furniture of her body into something nonthreatening. "You're right. I'll discuss this with the physician. I'll take my seat now."

The official smile returned. The receptionist's body relaxed. The flickering holograms settled into an even, untroubled flow.

Pre turned her back on the desk. She paused, looking around at the other people in the waiting room. To a person, they sat in a relaxed position, their palms were lying open on their thighs, their eyes only taking in the holoregisters that flashed and flickered and spun. No one's eyes met hers. No one seemed to even have noticed the exchange with the receptionist. But they must have, they would have, wouldn't they? Because those Implants not only displayed—they recorded. What were they recording now?

Slowly, carefully, she walked away. Out through the doorway. Down the bright, narrow hallway. Past the entry guards, who didn't seem to be looking for her yet. Into the sharp light of morning. She wondered if people with Implants could walk away. The movement of muscles was, after all, just electrical

impulses. Could the Implants be used to stop you? To para-
lyze you? To hold you in place?

She didn't know where she was going. But she could keep
walking, so she did.

***

At some point, Pre looked up and realized she was in
unfamiliar streets. She'd never been in this neighborhood
before—it was an old part of the city. The walking surfaces
were broken-up, cracked, uneven. There were odd arcs of
stain on the buildings—something between a charcoal
residue and a mildew infestation. The streets were too narrow
for Transports, and even narrower alleys branched off all too
often. It was a neighborhood of foot traffic, a neighborhood
of hiding places.

Reset coordinates? said her own voice in her head. Except of
course it wasn't her own voice. It was Qua. She hadn't even
noticed the jab of connection.

Where have you been? She she thought angrily at the robot,
though it wasn't the robot she was angry at. She should have
checked on Qua before now.

Qua answered, or showed her what Pre thought was an
answer. Images. Some of them came from advertisements. So
many types of clothing, so much intricate jewelry to choose
from. A set of plain sandals next to another set of plain
sandals. Do you want it in blue or red? Did you want jollof
rice or coconut rice with your balangu? Some images came
from entertainments. A person puts aside personal interest
for duty. A person chooses violence against another. A person
chooses which person they desire. Then changes their mind,
desires another. Desires someone who does not desire them.
From a list of texts in the data, a child chooses a text, reads it.
Chooses another. Which texts did she choose?

It was your decision, the robot seemed to be saying. If you'd wanted to go ahead with the Implants, I wouldn't have stopped you.

She decided, just for now, not to cry. She was standing in unfamiliar streets. She would not cry.

Reset coordinates? the little robot queried again. It emerged from her sleeve and climbed out to ride on her hand.

She couldn't go home. She knew that, in the sick pit of her stomach.

She also knew that they couldn't track her, not using Qua. It was something the engineers had been worried about from the beginning—the Familiars being used as location chips, turning every person who used one into their own private homing beacon. They dealt with it by scrambling the signal—each time the Familiar contacted the data stream, it did so using a rapidly shifting protocol, generating false and random location signifiers. The Familiars ricocheted in and out of the data like excited electrons, appearing and disappearing and reappearing unpredictably.

But if she returned to her usual paths, they would find her again. They would take away Qua, and they would fill her body with machinery that made her theirs.

Even so—no more home meant no more Subomi. No more home meant leaving behind her parents' Familiars. She would never know what they were thinking that day when their hearts stopped.

She supposed she never would have.

It occurred to her that she was making a target of herself, standing in the walkway. People walked past and around her, and here in the old part of the city, she could see a few people wearing Familiars openly, though she did notice the robots were damaged or in ill repair. Still, even here there were the Implanted. Even here, the Implants could use the eyes of the people walking by to identify and locate her. That man, there—were his unfocused eyes actually reporting her presence?

She started walking again, almost running. She had to get out of sight. She had to find somewhere that she couldn't be observed.

But there were so many alleyways, branching off, into dim mystery.

Which way? Which way?

Left, said Qua with a shimmer.

So she went left.

\*\*\*

The robot guided her down a honeycomb of alleys, further and further away from the populated streets. The walkways were increasingly narrow, the walls of the surrounding buildings nearer and nearer. The smell of the alleys changed; stale air was laced with rot and refuse. There were points where she had to turn sideways to pass between two buildings, like thread being pulled through a needle. Then the last alley opened to a small yard, lit by sun high above, shining down through the vertical vent made by the surrounding buildings. At the far end of the yard, she saw the skeletal remains of an abandoned factory. Qua reported that it had once housed machinery to fabricate Transport parts, before tax incentives had persuaded its owners to move their business outside the city. The large double-doors that served as entrance were held shut with a chain as thick as Pre's arm, not rusted through enough yet to be weak. The building's wide empty window frames held here and there the remnants of glass. Sharp teeth in so many gaping mouths.

Qua recommended that she climb in through one of those broken windows, so she did.

The sunlight from high above the yard streamed a good way

into the building—it did not hurt that the high roof above was punctured in places, so more light got in. She picked her way among the abandoned machinery, the gargantuan shelves of parts waiting to be assembled. She found a space, under a worktable, against one of the far back walls. It was a good hiding place, because she would be in the dark, but the area around her was well-lit. She could see someone approaching. She would not be surprised.

She climbed under and curled up, holding Qua in close to her chest, shielded by both of her hands. And then she cried herself to sleep.

***

She never knew if the guards found her because the system had correlated all the data from all the Implants she'd passed during her flight, or if the guards were simply surveying the factory routinely. After all, it was one thing for the factory owners to abandon the machinery because it wasn't worth the cost of moving it, but it was another thing entirely for the neighbors to attempt to salvage what had been left behind, to rescue it for reuse. No, that was thievery, and had to be prevented. There was a reason that she'd had machinery to hide behind after years of abandonment.

All she knew was she was dreaming one moment—hummingbirds had surrounded her, hummingbirds that she hadn't seen since she was a child, a cloud of jewels that darted and danced around her head—and then she was being hauled out from under the worktable, into the harsh light of halogen headlamps.

She couldn't help it—Qua fell from her hands as she was dragged. She prayed the little robot woke quickly enough to deploy its limbs before it smashed against the concrete floor.

Large gloved hands held her upright, immobilized. The light mounted on the guard's head shone directly in her eyes, and she blinked away, trying to look only at the soothing dark. Night had come, and the factory was otherwise pitch black.

In a low, bored voice, the guard said, "Identifying."

How considerate of his Implants to give her a status report.

There seemed to be two more guards, behind the one who held her. At least, there were two more sources of painful light.

"Ekwensi, P. Trespassing. Among other crimes, I'd think."

The hands dropped her, and she fell backward onto the concrete. She felt like she was falling forever, but then she landed so hard, so hard. She hadn't hit her head, though. That was something.

The head lamp's focus ranged over the ground around her, until it settled on a single location. There was Qua, lying unmoving on its side, sparkling in the spotlight.

The guard made a sound of disgust. He lifted his leg with its heavy boot.

"Why would you do that?" he said, almost to himself. "Why would you keep a part of yourself separate?"

He was bringing his foot down on Qua, then, his boot with the steel-enforced sole.

Pre heard the impact, the crunch and the squeal of metal against concrete, and all she could do was scream.

It was at that moment the Familiars swarmed.

The lights of the two far guards went out in a single flare, at the same time Pre heard the men yelp in pain. Then a chattering, clicking wave emerged from darkness into the light of the remaining guard's headlamp. The robots—hundreds of them—climbed the remaining guard's legs like rising water, their metal reflecting the last of his light in sparkles that jumped from dark surface to dark surface.

Pre heard him cry out, a deep guttural sound. Then he fell, or the robots gently lowered him, working as a single organism. He wasn't dead. They weren't killing him. But he landed on the ground, seizing, kicking out, his arms flailing. His lamp swung back and forth, the beam strafing the darkness.

A gentle light came on then, a warm, glowing brightness. Pre realized another crowd of Familiars surrounded her, and they'd all switched their eyes on full brightness, and from this sweet, collective light she could see. She scrambled forward toward the wreckage that had been Qua. There were almost no noises she could make that seemed right, that seemed to voice her grief, but she tried them all out anyway.

A voice from behind her said, "Gather it up. We can fix it."

She knew that voice. She looked up into Subomi's eyes.

"But you –" she said.

"I know," said Subomi, "But that was just camouflage." She leaned over and ran her hand tenderly over Pre's head. It was the most human affection Pre had had in years.

***

What was the conspiracy? Nothing more than those in power retaining their power—or consolidating it. Pre supposed that, from a certain angle, she too was part of a conspiracy now, being part of the Resistance, but in this case it was a conspiracy of the masses, not the advancement of a select selfish few.

The Familiars and the people who worked with them did fix Qua. Luckily, the robot's processor and memory crystals had been undamaged. It was hard for the Resistance to get parts, of course, but they rigged up what repairs they could. They couldn't replace the robot's right eye, or quite fix that wonky bend in its tail. It lost some of its sense of balance. It couldn't scramble quite as nimbly as it used to, climbing into its favorite place next to Pre's neck. But it didn't seem to mind if Pre helped it out, lifting it into place, making sure it was steady.

Every night, she laid it in the makeshift shrine in whatever small corner of that night's hideout she could claim. She laid it next to her parents' Familiars, which Subomi had managed to bring with her when she fled the flats. Pre let Qua have a moment beside those precious, silent bodies—the other Familiars had confirmed that they would always be silent, there was no way inside that data, there was no way back. She didn't bother to sort out whether it was she or Qua who was more comforted by this brief moment of proximity, of remembrance. When enough time had passed, she scooped Qua up gently, so gently, and took it with her to bed, where the robot divided its time between nestling its damaged head against Pre's ear and spooning contentedly with Subomi's Familiar.

# HALFWAY UP AND HALFWAY DOWN AND NOWHERE AT ALL

## Juliet Kemp

Juliet Kemp lives and writes in London, UK, with her partners, son, and dog. She believes that free time is very important and is constantly baffled by the fact that she never has any. She makes up for this by drinking a lot of tea. She has had stories published in several anthologies and online magazines, and blogs at http://julietkemp.com.

Mali glanced down to check her next foothold, careful not to look beyond it to the street, three storeys down. She settled her toe into it, then pushed up and grabbed at the window-ledge.

"Why do you still insist on doing this?" Nick complained. "If you'd stop being so stubborn…"

She jerked slightly as he spoke, missed, and hung from her other hand. "Shut. Up."

"Mali, come on. This is stupid, and dangerous."

"It's a lot more dangerous when you're distracting me." She got her feet back under her, pushed her toes down hard, then grabbed upwards again.

"But we're partners!"

"Not any more, we're not."

"You and me, buddies, the best team in the Southmarkets… Come on, Mali," Nick continued, oblivious.

Mali pulled herself up on the window-ledge, walking her feet upwards, until she could get her feet up onto the ledge. When she stood up, her nose was almost touching the window-glass, and the thick red curtains were closed, just as Jackson had promised.

"Shall I sort out the window?" Nick asked brightly, from where he was floating in mid-air behind her. She did her best to ignore the faint tracery of supporting magic that hung in the air underneath him. She wasn't a hedge-witch. She couldn't see magic. She didn't want to think about magic, or have anything to do with magic.

"Nick. If you don't bugger off right this second, I'm going to pin your ear to a drainpipe."

"Fine. Fine. I know when I'm not wanted." He paused. "We could talk about it once you're down?"

"Gods. Anything to get rid of you. Half an hour, in the Rose and Thorn. Get mine in."

Nick sighed gustily behind her, then there was silence.

***

Her payoff from Jackson jingled in her pocket as she walked into the Rose and Thorn. Nick was in their usual corner, with two glasses on the scratched table.

Mali slid onto the bench, and bumped his shoulder companionably. For a moment, it was like a hundred other evenings after a job. But Nick was thinner now, and his sleeves were pulled down right past his wrists.

"So," he said, pushing a glass towards her. "Let us discuss taking advantage of the advantages that are available to you." He grinned at her, eyes slightly too bright.

"Not interested," she said bluntly.

"Mali!"

He sounded just like when she'd first met him, two years ago. Just after she'd escaped. She'd been new, and lost, and terrified. Nick had taken her under his wing, cheered her up, and been truly impressed with her climbing. The first job they'd done, he'd used just that shocked tone of voice to talk her out of her share of the gains. Then he'd made a pass at her; but once past that awkwardness, they'd made a good team. Nick and Mali, cat-burglary a speciality.

"Magic swallows you up, Nick. Look at you. How many pounds have you lost since you started doing this?"

Three months. Only three months. A month to realise he was doing it, a month to realise he wasn't going to stop for her asking, and a month since she'd left him to it.

"I've always been skinny!"

"Not that skinny. Not to mention..." She grabbed his wrist and shoved his sleeve up. Neat parallel scars ran up the inside of his arm. More than she'd expected, for just three months. Nick jerked his hand away and glared at her, pulling his sleeve back down.

"Just spelling, or selling?" she asked.

He scowled and looked away.

"Both," she concluded. "How long you gonna be able to keep that up?"

The blood banks would buy a pint or two of anyone's blood, and sell it on, to the hedge-witches in the Southmarket, or to the Society on the other side of the river. Non-humans got double rates; magic-users triple. But if you sold it, you couldn't use it yourself, not safely. Nick never did have any sense.

"That's my business, okay?" Nick said. "Look, Mali, I'm not asking you to start using magic, if you're that against it. I'm just sayin', why not let me mind my own business, and come back and work with me? We've always done well together, right?"

"Not gonna take advantage of you doing that to yourself," Mali said, arms folded.

"C'mon, Mali," he wheedled. "Just give it a go. Just one job…"

She sighed. Maybe —maybe, if they did a job, he'd have a bit of cash. He wouldn't stop using it himself; but maybe he'd stop selling, at least for a bit.

He'd saved her once, though she'd never told him what she was running from; then they'd both looked out for each other. Maybe it was her turn to save him. Maybe she'd just given up too easily before. Maybe this was still home, the two of them, the way it had been.

"Right. Yeah. One job. You got something in mind?"

He looked slightly sheepish. "Well, yeah, I said to Ariadne…"

Mali shook her head, stomach twisting as her brief flare of hope died. "No way. Not anything for that fricking blood-dealer."

If Nick was getting jobs from Ariadne, he wasn't just a thief using a little magic any more. Ariadne was a strong hedge-witch in her own right, who only ran magic jobs —which was why Mali had always steered well clear of her —and she expected a lot. She'd been in the business a long, long time. Mali wouldn't —she couldn't —get that far in. The storm-clouds of her memories swirled, threatening.

"Seriously, Mali, it'd be perfect for us…"

"Drop it," she said. She downed her beer and stood up, trying to keep her knees steady. "You ever go back to regular thiev-ing, you let me know, yeah? Take care of yourself, Nick."

She wanted, desperately, to run, from Nick and magic and all the lurking memories, but she kept herself to a walk. You couldn't run from memories. You could only put them way, way down, and keep them there.

When she got home, she lay in bed and cursed herself for a fool. She should never have stayed this long. Sure, when she first met Nick, she'd run out of other options; but after that, she could still have gone. But by then Nick had been her friend, her first ever friend. And it had felt like safety here, in the alleys of Southmarket, where Mali who climbed and stole and was utterly magic-free could never be recognised as... She cut off the thought.

Nick wasn't safe any more. This wasn't home any more. But she knew more, now, than she had two years ago. Tomorrow. Tomorrow, she would buy herself some papers, good ones, and she would walk out of the gate and away from this damned magic-drenched city.

When she finally slept, her dreams were full of the tingle of magic, the flicker of candles, the metallic smell of blood pooling under her feet. She half-woke time and again, tangled in the sheet and sweating, then woke fully, finally, with the pre-dawn just showing through the shutters. She frowned up at the ceiling, trying to play back the noise that had awoken her, then got up. She'd just cast an eye outside, just to reassure herself.

She eased the door open a little, peered through, and gagged.

On the ground outside was Nick. Pale, blood-drained, and very definitely dead.

***

She wasn't sure how she got to Ariadne's. It was a series of snapshots: clothes, bringing Nick—Nick's body—inside, rousing her neighbour to come and sit with him. She couldn't bear that he would be alone. Her rage was a cold fire as she banged on Ariadne's door. She might never have been here before, but you could hardly live in the Southmarket and not know where Ariadne was.

"Nick's dead," she said, when the older woman opened the door.

Ariadne shrugged. "Don't look at me, dearie, it wasn't my doing. And you would be his...?"

"We worked together. Before he used magic. And it was your doing. You sent him," Mali said. Her throat felt swollen inside.

"I offered him a job, dearie," Ariadne said. "You worked with Nick; will you tell me you've never done anything with risk?"

Mali took a ragged breath, and stepped inside. Ariadne stood back to let her past, eyeing her curiously. Inside, a neat workbench stood against the wall, with jars and bottles and pouches lining the shelves above it. The only other furniture was a battered chair by the fireplace with a faded quilt crumpled on the seat, and a large, solid chest.

"His blood's been taken," Mali said.

She wanted to say that that wouldn't happen on the sort of job she took, but they would both know that for a lie. You could wind up dead just walking down the street round here, never mind thieving; and there was always a blood dealer who'd pay for a barely-breathing body and turn it into a drained, unbreathing one without asking too many questions of the vendor.

It could have happened. But it never had happened, not when it was Mali and Nick and no damn magic at all.

"Like I say, dearie. He knew the risks. And the rewards."

"Did you get it offered to you?"

Ariadne scowled. "There's no need to be rude, even if you are grieving. I don't deal in death. You know that."

Mali swallowed, and ducked her head.

Ariadne looked her up and down, eyes narrowing, then pulled a knife out of her apron pocket and sliced it shallowly across her forearm. She had a thick patchwork of scars, both old and barely scabbed over. Ariadne ran her fingers over the cut, tilted her head slightly, then wiped the knife on her apron and dropped it back into her pocket, frowning.

"Interesting."

"I don't do magic," Mali said.

"I know that, dearie. But you could. Oh, you could. There's something about you…"

She reached towards Mali, and Mali jumped back, suddenly alert. She did not want Ariadne to see anything more about her.

"I said, I don't do magic."

"Why are you here then, dearie?" Ariadne asked sharply. "Your friend died, and that I'm sorry for, but it wasn't my doing. Try the Watch, if you're looking for answers."

Mali scoffed. "Yeah, like I want the Watch turning me upside down and shaking me."

Ariadne shrugged. "It's life-blood. The Society would be happy to deal with it and have no interest in anything else." She was watching Mali intently.

Mali raised an eyebrow and hoped Ariadne didn't see her shiver. "I don't like magic. That don't mean I want to let the Society loose down here. Wouldn't have thought you would either."

The Society weren't known for their subtlety. Which was why the blood-dealers, and their clients, continued to exist; the cure was worse than the disease. And if the Watch would turn her upside down and shake her, the Society would turn her head inside-out as well while they were at it, and then, well. She wouldn't do that.

Ariadne shrugged. "I've survived the Society and their little games this long. Just wanted to know if I should be tidying up." She turned away to put another log on the fire.

Mali's fury had ebbed a little, and she took a deep breath

that felt like the first since she'd woken. Why was she here? She was looking for someone to blame for Nick's death, and Ariadne had sent him out. But, yes, her and Nick, they'd both taken on plenty of risk in their time, separately and together. Nick would be furious if she put this on Ariadne.

Who had killed him, then? Them, she could blame.

"What was the job he went on last night?"

"Well now, there's a thing," Ariadne said. "It wasn't my job at all, as it happens. Not last night. He came to say he couldn't do what he'd said he would, after all. I hadn't anything else, but someone came in from the Lines. Looking for Nick Shades, some customer of theirs asking for him. Nick was off quick as sixpence while I was still saying I was no one's messaging service." She spread her hands. "That's all I know."

If she'd said yes, last night, they'd have been on that other job, and Nick would still be safe. She could have kept him safe, and she hadn't.

It was too late now. But she would not let him go unavenged.

"I'd be careful with revenge, dearie," Ariadne said. "It doesn't always end up how you'd expect. But who am I to offer you advice?"

She turned away, busying herself with something on the workbench at the side of the room, then spoke without turning round.

"Funny thing is, that first job, they asked for him by name, too. I wouldn't have said Nick was that well known, myself. But money buys you foibles, doesn't it."

"Thank you," Mali said, and turned away, the fury a burning-cold weight in her guts.

***

A tram rattled overhead, smoke belching behind it, as she

stepped onto the Tall Bridge's suspended walkway, joining the folk of all species walking north to jobs on the good side of the city, passing the night-shift cleaners yawning their way back again.

She glanced down at the river and frowned. Why had Nick's body fetched up on her doorstep, and not down there? Who would have bothered, but not wake her? Her pace slowed. In memory, the dark spectre of the Baron moved behind the flickering of the candles...

No. If the Baron knew where she was, she'd be back there already. She'd escaped. She was fine. Someone had found Nick and not wanted to explain themselves to her, that was all. Everyone had known Nick and Mali. Her eyes prickled again.

What mattered was avenging him, not idle speculation. She walked faster.

At the end of the bridge, one set of tramlines dipped steeply to the embankment, and the other set carried on towards Two-Storey Station. Underneath it, opposite the steep stairs down from the walkway, was The Lines.

The exterior that looked trendily down-at-heel at night just looked shabby in the morning light. The Lines combined drinking den and introductions bureau: to people who could provide supplies, do small spells, handle this or that little magical job for you. White-shading-to-grey, at its darkest. You wouldn't find anyone dealing in life-blood in the Lines; not even vein-blood these days, with the blood-banks so easy. Just folk using this charm and that to increase the power they got of themselves. The tingle of spell that hung around the place made Mali's back crawl.

Round the back, the kitchen door was open. A lizard in an apron and a grubby vest was sweeping up, ignoring a short human with elaborate tattoos who was lecturing an invisible audience, hands waving.

The tattooed man broke off and looked at her, eyebrow raised. "Yes? What can I do for you, then?"

She reminded herself, firmly, that she just wanted information. No one at the Lines would deliberately get involved in something like this; not over this side of the city, with the Society so near at hand.

"You sent someone over to Ariadne, over the river, last night. After Nick Shades, for a job."

Tattooed man eyed her narrowly, arms folded. "What of it? Perfectly legal and none of your damn business. He turned up, they went off, nowt to do with us."

"Nick fetched up on my doorstep this morning," Mali said. "All drained and white and dead. You know anything about that?"

"Nick? Really? Gods. Poor kid." He shook his head. "I swear, this city's getting worse by the day."

"You had nothing to do with it?"

"With Nick? Of course not." He scowled at her. "What do you take me for?"

"Who was it, though?" she pressed. "Who asked for him? How come they were asking you?"

"I figured Nick was moving up in the world," the tattooed man said, rubbing the back of his neck. "Y'know, starting to get a reputation. Good luck to him, I figured. Gods. Poor kid."

"Who was it, then?" she asked again.

"We don't discuss clients," the tattooed man said automatically, then looked at her, swallowed hard, and put his hands up. "We don't! You know we don't! But truth is, I've no idea anyway. Full cloak, deep hood. Very tacky, if you ask me, but effective."

The lizard, leaning on his broom, snorted. "Couldn't you tell, Jake? Was a Sorcerer. Sorcerer wanting hooked up with some half-arsed street wizard —sorry, girlie, but it's true. Embarrassing."

Jake shrugged, his ink rippling with the movement. "It happens from time to time. When they don't fancy dirtying their own hands."

"They went off together?" Mali asked.

Jake nodded. "Had a quick chat and left. No sign of any coercion, before you ask, and the client paid the connection fee on the way out. All legit and above-board."

"Thanks," she said flatly. "I guess I'll go try the Society, then."

Jake snorted. "What, just knock on the front door and say hey, any of your lot out at the Lines last night? You'll be taking bits of you home in a bucket." He shook his head. "You take my advice, you'll leave it. Whatever trouble Nick got himself into, it's a damn shame, but you gotta look after your own hide, yeah?"

She looked at him, and he threw up his hands. "Whatever. Good luck."

Back out in the alleyway she stood, unsure. A Sorcerer. Jake was right; she could get in easily enough, but how was she going to find the right person?

Someone coughed, and she whirled round. The lizard was there, pulling a small velvet bag out of the pocket of his apron.

"Here. That Sorcerer had a drink, last night."

Mali cautiously took the bag and peered into it to see a glass with a sticky residue at the bottom of it.

"But he had gloves, right?" she said.

The lizard shook his head. "No gloves. Stupid. Had him down for a student. Jumpy. Careless. Figured could find him, worth a few units not to tell his master where he'd been. Been and left proof, no less." He shook his head disapprovingly. "There it is, if you've someone who can use it."

"Yes," Mali said, quietly. "I have. Thanks." She tucked the bag away in a pocket. "Do you want something for it?"

The lizard shrugged, and shook his head. "Nah. Take it. Nick was a good kid. Can't be doing with Sorcerers."

He flicked his tongue out in disgust, then left. Mali looked at the bag.

\*\*\*

The Society complex, a warren of buildings of different ages and styles built around two connected quadrangles, was west of the Lines, further from the river. The streets here were wider, and more regularly swept, and Mali didn't know them well. She began to feel conspicuous; but she didn't want to wait. She ducked her head slightly and did her best to look like a servant out on an errand.

Around the Society itself, though, the houses were smaller again. Rich folk wouldn't live this close to it; those who did were generally involved in tending to the needs of Sorcerers and their apprentice-students. Ingredients, bookstalls, healers, food-hawkers, the odd eatery. No hedge-witches round here; just like Sorcerers stayed away from the Southmarket.

Rumour had it that a sufficiently talented hedge-witch could apply as an apprentice. Mali'd never heard of it happening for real. Sorcerers were here, hedge-witches were there, and that was that. Money talked in magic like it did in anything else. The Nicks of this world would never walk through the Society gates, regardless of their dream-tales. Mali's dream-tales didn't involve going anywhere near the Society; but then, this wasn't a dream-tale, and she wouldn't be using the gates.

A couple of streets away from the Society itself was the alleyway she was looking for, with its convenient drainpipe. The Society held that any Sorcerer who couldn't protect their own person and belongings was better off without either, so threw no wards around the complex. Mali knew the route in by description —knowledge was useful, so she'd bartered with a couple of acquaintances who worked in this area —but she'd never run it herself. Too much magic to be safe. Too risky if they caught her. She repressed a shiver. She would just have to not get caught.

She followed the circuitous route around the higgeldy-piggeldy rooftops and their inconvenient mix of heights and street-widths. As she got to the complex itself, her teeth itched with the magic oozing from the stones, humming and fizzing, wound through the buildings over the centuries.

When she reached the student quarters, after a couple of minutes and one particularly awkward move, she crouched for a moment to catch her breath. Slowly, she pulled the bag out of her pocket, then stopped, hand shaking. She was Mali now, and Mali didn't use magic. Then she thought of Nick's body, white-cold on her doorstep, and her chin went up.

This was a tool. It was once, once only, just for this.

Teeth set, she drew her knife swiftly across her left forearm. She wiped her right-hand fingers across the cut, and reached into the bag for the glass. She could feel something already where her fingers left bloody fingerprints on the glass, but for good measure she waited until another drop of blood had gathered, and let it fall into the glass.

Around her, the lines of magic leapt to life, a tracery of colour across the stones shining brighter than the mid-morning sunlight. It told her already, written in light, that Nick had never been here. She concentrated instead on the glass.

The image of the person who had held it took shape in her mind. Her sight plummeted down through one, two, three floors, following a yellow-blue shimmering thread, before she saw him, dozing on a narrow student bed, a book open on his skinny chest. She fixed the location in her mind, and dropped the glass back into the bag. She expected the magic to fade, but she could still see it; the shining tracery of the old magic in the stones, and that yellow-blue thread. She shivered.

You could, dearie, you could.

This was for once. Just for once. This wasn't her, it wasn't for her. This was for Nick. She pushed any other thoughts back down into darkness.

She found a window to slide through, and followed the thread downwards and down a flight of stairs, to the door she wanted. The lock was barely worth the bother of picking. She hesitated for a moment, looking at the apprentice, the magic telling her that she could just pick the information from his mind. It would be easy. Easy.

She got her knife to his throat just as he woke up.

"I... what the..." he spluttered, the book falling to the floor. Then he took a breath, and Mali saw the lines of magic bend.

"I really wouldn't," she said, mildly. "You think one more thought like that, and I'll know." She pressed a little harder with the knife.

This incompetent child hadn't killed Nick. He just had information. And after that, it was embarrassingly easy to extract it. He hadn't known who had paid him, just what they wanted: Nick Shades ("some street wizard", she saw the thought behind his eyes) to a particular location. The money was good. It didn't sound arduous. Nick had been alive when he left.

"You know who sent you," Mali said, bone-certain.

"They told me not to ask. They told me."

His eyes darted around. Mali waited.

"Shit! It was Proctor Gideon. We did this spell in class, I shouldn't have, I... Whoever it was, they were sent by Proctor Gideon."

It took all Mali's self-control not to move a muscle.

"But he said I mustn't tell anyone... oh gods."

"Don't worry," Mali said. "I'll make sure no one can trace it back to you." One way or another.

*** 

Mali waited for nightfall in a cobbler's disused attic, jumping every time the shop's bell jingled under her feet.

Proctor Gideon. The Baron's secretary. The Baron. She shivered, compulsively, memories of Gideon's sharp sardonic face flickering in her head. But, surely, surely, it must be Gideon working off his own bat, though then how in the hells had Nick had gotten involved? But Nick never did have much sense. Maybe he was just collateral damage, unrelated.

It couldn't possibly be anything to do with her. Just coincidence. Gideon had his fingers in plenty of pies. If he knew where she was then the Baron would know, and then she'd be back there already.

She had to avenge Nick. Nothing else mattered. She felt hollow around the anger, hollow all the way out to her skin.

At least she knew how to get in. She'd got out, after all.

It was well past midnight, the coldest and the slowest part of the night, when she made her way up the castle wall. It wasn't easy. She hadn't expected it to be easy. But the tiny footholds in the nearly-smooth wall were enough, and tonight, she had the ice-cold nerve that had sometimes eluded her. She knew, as if she were being told, which hold to use. She moved up the wall like a dancer, and told herself that all the practice had finally paid off. She ignored Ariadne's voice in her head.

She knew exactly where she was going. Once there, she paused below Gideon's window, and used her free hand to slice across her arm. It felt almost as if the threads of magic that sprang into view, outlining the wards, had already been in her vision.

She peered through the window. The curtains were open, but the room was dark, and the bed was empty.

He must be in his office. Gideon had never seemed to need much sleep. It had an outside window, but it would be faster to go through than around. She found a corridor window, with weaker wards, which she melted away with fingertips dabbed with blood. Even corridor wards weren't that weak. But then, she knew already what was in her blood.

She had to avenge Nick. Nothing else mattered. Nick had saved her, and she hadn't saved him, and now he was dead. She owed him.

The office door was unwarded. She took a deep breath, hefted her dagger in her hand, and walked in.

*** 

The room was dark, lit only by a magelight on the opposite wall. Mali saw a silhouette at the desk. Gideon, it must be Gideon, and she was bringing her arm up, just scare him, she wanted answers first... Then the door behind her slammed shut, and her eyes finished adjusting, and her arm hiccoughed and halted.

Not Gideon. The Baron.

Memory crashed in and swirled around her, blood and candlelight and misery.

"I knew you'd come back eventually," he said, sounding satisfied.

There was a beaker of blood —Nick's blood —on the desk in front of him. Mali pulled herself out of her remembered panic.

"You killed Nick," she said, and threw.

She'd never thrown to kill before, but the knife met his chest exactly where she'd aimed. The Baron shook his head at her, disapproving, and the honed point skittered down his chest, scoring through the fabric. He caught the knife before it could clatter to the floor.

"Really," he said, "you have been socialising with quite inappropriate people during your absence."

He dipped his fingers in the beaker, then shook them across the floor. He got up and she tried desperately to move, to run, but her feet were rooted to the floor.

He came towards her, and took her chin between his fingers. She could feel the tingle from the blood on his other hand — Nick's, Nick's blood —resonating more strongly now it was closer to her, and her stomach turned at the metallic smell. She stared at the Baron, hatred rising through her, but still she couldn't move.

"I made you," he said softly. "You cannot stand against me."

He had made her. With blood and bone and magic, to channel more magic. Her first memories were confused, flashes of light and darkness, of an all-body ache that she couldn't escape. Then the clearer memories, standing in the middle of the ritual chamber, over and over again, surrounded by a ring of thick white candles as tall as her, and the Baron moving in the shadows beyond the candlelight, tipping a beaker onto the floor until the thick liquid ran down to touch her bare feet, and the tingling of magic filled her. Afterwards she would be sick and shaking in her room for days, as the resonance in her bones and blood strengthened again.

Slowly, over time, she'd worked it out. A half-envious comment from Gideon, a strong Sorcerer himself; the magical principles he was teaching her; that ritual chamber and the nothing before it. Cryptic comments from the Baron whenever he returned her to that candle-lit circle.

The Baron had made her, of blood and bone and stolen life. She had known, then, that her magic already outstripped Gideon, even if he wouldn't teach her to use it. She had known, finally, that the Baron was creating her to control that ability, to join with him in his castings and increase his power beyond all resistance.

She had run. Out of a window, and halfway down the wall it occurred to her to wonder how she knew how to climb. Who had known, before their blood was hers? For a moment she'd nearly opened her hands and let herself drop. But she hadn't chosen how she'd come to be, and she couldn't change it. All she could do was to live with it.

She couldn't see how to climb the city wall, ten metres of spelled-slick granite always under watch, and the gates meant papers she didn't have. Then she'd fallen in with Nick, and by the time she could have got them, she'd believed herself safe. Or chosen to; she hadn't wanted to leave that first experience of friendship, of something that felt like home. Stupid.

Desperately, now, she struggled again to run. The Baron's will surrounded her, and after a moment she sagged slightly in his grip.

The Baron nodded approvingly, and let go. He looked down at the hilt of the knife in her boot, and dismissed it with a shrug. Mali's teeth ground together, but she couldn't so much as reach towards it.

"Once you experience what we will undertake together, once

you feel the magic, I assure you, my dear, you will agree it is more than worth any sacrifice."

He glanced over at the beaker on the desk. "It's poor quality, but then again, the relationship strengthens it. So perhaps all this trouble was for the best after all."

He turned to walk back towards the desk, and Mali snarled.

Sacrifice. As if he ever made sacrifice of himself. The bare handful of scars on the Baron's arms were decades old, from his very first forays into magic, before he was strong enough to use only power from others. Mali looked at the beaker on his desk and swallowed against nausea. Her fault. Her fault.

Her anger was growing, uncoiling, as her breathing quickened and her fingertips tingled. The tangled lines of magic around the room shone brighter.

If only she had her knife. If only she could do something, anything... Magic sang through her blood, echoing inside her skull.

"If I'd known how straightforward it would be to bring you back," the Baron said over his shoulder, "I would have arranged it far earlier. Still, perhaps your time outside has done you good. We shall see."

The tingle spread up her arms, down her legs, under every inch of her skin. The anger burnt hot now, and she breathed sharply into it and felt the Baron's will shake off her like water from a hot pan. As he turned, his mouth opening in surprise, her knife flew up into her hand, and she threw it straight at his neck.

It slid into him this time as if it had been magnetised, and he crumpled sideways with a bubbling cry. The beaker fell to the floor and Nick's blood spread out under him, mingling with his own. Mali stood and watched, curiously, as he blinked at her, tried to say something. Asking? Threatening? Then his mouth fell open, and his eyes rolled back, and he died.

She staggered sideways as the magic lines wound through the room shuddered with earthquake violence. The guards would be here soon. She supposed she should feel something, joy or terror or some emotion she couldn't think of. But for a moment, it seemed that she could once again no longer move, nor even think. Perhaps, as the Baron's creation, she would die with him.

She wasn't sure how long that moment of suspended animation lasted. Then someone thumped on the door, and her mind moved again.

The trouble was, she had no idea how to get out. She hadn't planned for leaving, even when she'd thought it was just Gideon. She hadn't really planned at all. She'd never make it down from the balcony, not with guards everywhere.

She walked across to the Baron's body to retrieve her knife from his neck, then stopped and looked down at the blood on her hands.

No. Not that. Something ticked in her head, something about when she'd broken free. Dirt on her hands, no blood left, and the Baron's shock... No blood. She had had no blood on her hands, and she had used magic anyway.

She could hear axe-strokes on the other side of the door. She crossed the room to the basin of water stood against the wall. She poured water over her hands, again and again, blood and water cascading to the floor, then raised them in front of her face, turning them over. Clean.

She was magic. Built of magic, made from magic. Magic and blood and bone. She hadn't asked for it, hadn't wanted it, hadn't chosen to be made; but she couldn't change it. She had run from it for two years, but what was the point in that? Not using it wouldn't help, her or anyone else.

But never again with blood. Hers or anyone else's.

She turned to the balcony, and flung the glass doors open.

The sun was just rising on the horizon, its light bathing her as she climbed onto the balcony rail and balanced there. Below her, she could see the city, and the sparkle of the river's curve. She'd never been afraid above the ground.

The door of the room splintered.

Mali spread her arms, hands full of her own power, and jumped into the sunrise.

# THE THIRD KIND

## Carrie Vaccaro Nelkin

Carrie Vaccaro Nelkin writes
short stories and poetry and
is author of the novel SNARE.
Visit her on Twitter @cvnelkin,
on Facebook (www.facebook.
com/cvnelkin), and on her
website, www.cvnelkin.com.

"There are two kinds of ghosts," Ray's Aunt Edith had told us. "You must never harm the first kind. The lost souls, even the angry ones who try to frighten you—they can't hurt anyone, though they may want you to think otherwise. You would be doing them a catastrophic disservice."

Catastrophic. I shivered as Ray and I entered the small house that sat a quarter-mile into the woods, its roof cupped by trees and ragged shade. Again I wondered if I'd lived a life before this one and died a catastrophic death, beset as I was since childhood by images of fatal crashes, drowning, lethal blows to the head—flashes of personal destruction too violent to be mere imagination. The images rarely repeated them-selves, instead mutated into variations on numerous themes, all of them leading to the same thought: One moment, one catastrophic moment is all it takes to decide your life.

I'd never mentioned this to anyone. Not even to Ray, my closest friend of twenty years who knew things about me that no one had any business knowing.

The living room smelled of earth and soot. I dropped my duffle bag on the floor and tried the nearest light switch. The bulb that turned on overhead did nothing but create new shadows and move the old ones.

"Let's get a fire going." Ray blew on her hands, her eyes

wandering the bleak walls before settling on the hearth. "There's wood in that bin."

I made her pick out the logs and kindling because I didn't want to touch anything that was living among the cobwebs. Then, as I watched her down on her knees reaching inside the chimney for the flue, I thought of what might be up there that could dive down and eat her hand.

"How can you harm a ghost?" she'd asked Edith. "They're immaterial. They're dead. You can't kill them again."

Edith had stopped stirring the coffee in front of her and stared at Ray under the bright kitchen fluorescents. "It depends on what kind they are. You can disbelieve in them. Disbelieving is different from not acknowledging. If you see one and convince yourself it isn't real, you kill a small piece that can never regenerate, and when enough people have done that, a sufficient portion of the spirit is gone so that it no longer has a chance to move on. Disbelief robs the ghost of an afterlife it's having trouble getting to." She'd resumed stirring, then said, "Please pass the milk," which I'd forgotten I was holding several inches above my cup, unpoured. "This applies only to the first kind, of course."

Now I tilted my watch to the light and brushed invisible dirt from it with the edge of my shirt. Whatever misgivings I had, and whatever Ray did or did not believe, we were here for Edith, though I wished we hadn't arrived before her and Mrs. Montoya. We'd come specifically to help rid the house of ghosts. Not the first kind. The second kind.

\*\*\*

We were checking out the dining room when Edith poked her head in. She wore an Irish fisherman's sweater under a barn coat, and her hair was full of twigs as though she'd walked through brambles. She leaned through the doorway just as I caught sight of the girl sitting at the table. The girl's sunken eyes and stringy hair struck me like a slap. I gasped, but neither Edith nor Ray noticed as they greeted each other. In seconds the girl was gone, and I knew I had seen my first ghost.

"Beth, dear." Edith kissed me on the cheek, smelling of cold fresh air and Shalimar. "Thank you so much for coming. But I'm afraid we have to leave and return tomorrow morning. Mrs. Montoya had a family emergency and can't get here until then. We shouldn't stay the night without her."

Ray pulled a chair out from the table and sat. "We're not safe without Mrs. Montoya?"

Edith regarded her niece a moment as if she were looking at a slow-witted puppy. "You need to start taking all of this seriously, or you'll put yourself and the rest of us in danger." Her head snapped up and she eyed the mirror hanging above the empty fireplace across the room. The face of the girl I'd just seen stared out from the mottled glass, changing quickly two, three, five, ten times into other faces before disappearing. Edith removed her wire-rim glasses and pinched the bridge of her nose.

"I saw her at the table just as you came in," I said.

Edith nodded. "It's all right. Let her be. Let them all be. She's not our concern today."

"Who are you talking about?" Ray spun her gaze around the room.

Edith placed a hand on her arm and said nothing.

"Why don't you just tear the place down?" Ray got up and followed Edith to the living room, hands jingling change in the pockets of her jacket. "Reduce it to splinters. Whoever buys it is going to have to do that anyway. There's no way to refurbish it without spending a fortune."

"First of all, that's not true." Edith's tone was unequivocal. I imagined she sounded much as she did when addressing students who were recalcitrant. "And even if it were, this house is of value to me. I'm not going to be the one to raze it."

"It was in your husband's family a long time, wasn't it?" I offered.

She gave me a grateful look. "Yes. And demolishing it would be like stirring up a hornet's nest. Not because of those who've done no wrong by staying, who are just waiting to find their way. They would simply be forced to roam. The real danger is from the others."

The second kind. I swallowed, and found my throat dry. Now that I had seen the girl in the dining room, I had no doubt the other variety was real too.

*** 

"Unlike the first kind," Edith had told us, "these are corporeal. They are as solid to the touch as you and I are. It's what makes them hard to recognize. That, and the fact that sometimes they have difficulty speaking, though that in itself is not, of course, an infallible indicator."

"What makes them so dangerous?" I had asked that night in her apartment, cutting off the questions I saw brewing in Ray's eyes.

"They are not at all lost," she'd replied in her soft voice. It occurred to me she would make a good minister's wife if she ever remarried. "They have a purpose, and that is their continued existence, which can be obtained only by their removing the souls of the living and subsuming them into themselves. Once absorbed, your soul dies. It's not even imprisoned, with a slim chance of release should this ghost be destroyed. It is simply gone, burned off like coal in a furnace to power the being that stole it."

Ray had kicked me under the table then. I kicked her back.

"How do you know all this?" she asked. "And how can they be destroyed?"

Edith took a sip of coffee and put the cup down carefully in its saucer. "They have a dark spot at the back of their tongue, by the throat. It's the Devil's thumbprint, the ultimate sign of their identity."

Ray's fingers drummed on my thigh. She leaned forward. "But how do you know all this?"

"What do you think?"

"Mrs. Montoya? She's the only medium I've heard you talk about."

Edith's lips pursed. "She's more than a medium. And no, Mrs. Montoya has nothing to do with how I know."

"Okay." Ray sat back, folding her arms across her chest. "Have you ever seen one?"

Edith's face was suddenly weary. "Ray, if I had anyone else to ask, I would. But I need to clean the place out and sell it as soon as possible. You cannot go in there without taking me seriously. It's dangerous for you and for all of us. Yes, I've seen one. Two, actually. And I've seen what they can do. They're unable to leave the property unless they're properly exorcised—or destroyed. I have a responsibility to innocent, unsuspecting buyers. And to the realtors."

"And if you don't succeed?"

Edith's eyes fixed on the wall behind me, as if she hadn't heard her.

I touched Edith's hand across the table. "Would you abandon it?"

"Set it on fire?" Ray said. I frowned at her.

Edith squeezed my hand gently. "If I abandon the house, I'll be responsible for every death that occurs in it. Every vagrant. Every hiker seeking shelter. Every child who wanders in."

She turned to Ray. "If I burn it down I'll simply be releasing them into the world."

I heard myself breathing. Ray was very still.

Barely above a whisper I asked, "How do they take your soul?"

Edith pressed her fingers to her lips as if to stifle a cry. "They garner your immediate sympathy, like a stray dog or cat. The moment you offer compassion, in any form, spoken or not, physical or not, they will extend a hand to your heart and pull the life out of you. Just like that. They leave a shell, a dead husk." Her gaze drifted across the room as if viewing some long-buried scene.

Ray sat back, eyes narrowed. "So how do you kill them? Something to do with that black spot on their tongue?"

"No. You crack their skulls open."

***

"Beth! Help me put out the fire." Ray pulled at my arm and I came back to the present. "Come on. We need water."

I followed her to the kitchen, a dingy galley with cracked linoleum. "Where will we go?"

"That motel we passed. We just talked about it with Edith." She gave me a funny look and grabbed the empty teakettle that was on the stove. "Look for a big pot or a bucket, will you?"

"Where's your aunt?"

"Outside. Why?"

"Someone's in the living room."

Ray swiveled. "Where?" She crept to the doorway and looked around, then straightened up. "Let's hurry. I hate this place."

She filled the teakettle while I opened the cupboards. I found a heavy saucepan with a handle, and a box of salt that I almost dropped when a centipede crawled out from behind it. I tucked the salt under my arm and with both hands carried the pot full of water out of the kitchen. Ray had emptied the kettle into the fire and was returning for more water.

"Here, let me get that." She reached for the sauce pot.

"No, take the salt, it's about to fall."

She slipped it out from under my elbow. "We'll use this last." She put the box on the mantle and went back to the kitchen.

As I poured water over the diminished fire, a feeling of being watched bristled over me. I turned and saw a boy standing in the farthest corner, eight or nine years old, his beauty evident, even in the meager light. The shock of wavy hair and the striped tee shirt over jeans made me nostalgic for something indefinable. He receded into the shadows, luminous face and large dark eyes the last things visible. The questions jostled each other. What kind of ghost was he? Who had he been when alive? Was he a ghost? Could anyone dead be so exquisite?

There it was again, that sense of impending doom, as if I were hurtling toward a violent end, toward a scream cut short by a burst of pain or an explosion into nothing. I heard Ray running the faucet in the sink full force and wondered why Edith hadn't come back inside. The moment elongated. In slow motion I moved toward the kitchen.

Could ghosts conjure more ghosts, I wondered, or were they all loners?

I heard the gurgle before I understood what I was looking at: Ray pinned upright against the refrigerator, trembling, face hidden by something hunkered atop the freezer. Striped fabric rode up skinny ribs as the boy hunched over the edge in a pose no human could maintain, his upside-down face latched onto Ray's like a hyena's on a carcass, hands flat against her chest.

Ray gurgled, then began convulsing.

The moment broke. I swung the saucepan with both arms. It hit the boy's head with a clap and he swayed but didn't let go. I slammed it against his ribs, twice. A rush of wind flew out of his mouth, but no other sound as his grip loosened and he fell forward. He hit the floor seconds before Ray slumped to the linoleum.

I bent over her, unable to control my shaking. Her eyes were closed and her face was a mass of bleeding pinpricks, but she was breathing.

The boy stirred and I clutched the saucepan harder. I was both someone else and myself at my purest, my truest, my most focused as I struck his face with it. I dropped the pan and seized his head to smash it against the floor, once, twice, a third time until his eyes fluttered white and I felt the snap and splinter of an eggshell skull and the spittle running out of his mouth bloomed red. The hands I drew back did not look like mine.

"What's going on?" Edith's silhouette loomed above me in the doorway. The rusty shovel she held clattered to the floor as she knelt with a sound of distress. She cradled Ray's head, her own face gray in the stink and horror of the kitchen. She checked Ray's breathing, then reached into her pocket and threw me a small flashlight.

She indicated the boy. "Look in his mouth. Make sure."

I was paralyzed.

"Do it!"

I felt a million miles away. I could almost hear my muscles creak as I picked up the flashlight where it had rolled under the boy's arm. My reluctance to touch him rose at the coldness of his skin, but I took his jaws and stretched them open, averting my face at the smell that rose from his mouth. "There's blood."

Edited swooped her hand up to the counter for a roll of paper towels I hadn't noticed. I tore off a wad and bunched it into a thick cylinder.

"Don't get it on you." She helped Ray sit up.

I let the paper soak up what was in the boy's mouth and directed the beam at his throat. I sensed myself falling into an abyss. Any second now I would be swallowed by a darkness so great it would eclipse all life. I had just done something terrible. Yet there it was, a small but distinct black spot on the base of his tongue.

I sat back on my heels as my gut began to roil.

"Now do you understand why you had to do that?" Edith's voice still had a harsh edge. She glanced at the black liquid pooling on the floor. "He looks like a boy. He bleeds like a boy. He might have been one. But you need to remember always that you did not kill a boy."

\*\*\*

We left the body there. "We have to leave now," Edith said as we helped Ray to the car. "It'll attract others of his kind. Most likely it'll be gone by the time we return tomorrow."

Others of his kind. What would they do with the remains, I wondered, the thought a flicker without heat, a pulse that died before completion in a mind that couldn't comprehend what had just happened.

"The fire," I said.

"It's out." Edith buckled Ray into the passenger seat. Ray was awake but not alert. Edith asked me, "Are you sure you can drive?"

I nodded, the motion automatic and empty.

She said, kindly, "Just follow me, then. It's a mile down the road."

I drove with one hand and wiped tears and snot from my face with the other. I reached over to touch Ray and saw her cheeks glistening too.

I thought Ray would need medical attention. But she appeared to get back to normal gradually and insisted she felt fine after her facial wounds were disinfected. She remembered nothing of the incident itself, only that she had seen the boy at the kitchen door.

"He reminded me of someone." She inspected the marks on her face in the bathroom mirror. "I don't really want to go back."

That evening Edith ordered food from the diner next door and we sat in her room chewing without taste or appetite. Ray's only hunger was for information. She peppered her aunt with questions that carried none of the skepticism she'd showed when Edith first enlisted us. Who were the ghosts? Why two kinds? Were they all previous residents or could random ghosts appear? How long had the house been haunted?

Edith's answers hovered around me like wisps I couldn't quite grasp. ". . . early 1900s . . . she was stoned to death, then burned . . . your uncle Jack's great-great-grandfather . . . I don't know why two kinds, but there have always been . . . always. . . ."

I felt ill and floated into sleep while she was still talking. That night I ran a fever and couldn't stop trembling. My throat burned and the back of my tongue felt as if someone had dragged a rake over it. With Ray next to me on the thin mattress I dreamed—all night, it seemed—not of what I had done, not of fragile bone fracturing against metal or staining red, but of calamitous car crashes. I was always behind the wheel, colliding with concrete barriers, flying through the air in a twisting heap, crunching into bridge abutments, sliding down ravines into icy water, where I would feel the life drain from me even before my lungs filled. I had killed something that looked like a child. I'd been able to do it. I was capable of it. I hadn't hesitated one iota. One catastrophic moment. I had changed in one catastrophic moment.

The fact that it wasn't really a child didn't matter.

Toward morning I woke, drenched in sweat, to find Ray curled tightly around me, twitching, her legs thrusting against the back of my knees. I tried to loosen her arms but she only yanked me closer and I couldn't breathe. Her own breathing stopped, and for a good thirty seconds she was still, no inhaling, no exhaling, in a silence as frightening as her previous tumult. I pulled her arms off me and immediately she crushed me in her embrace again. The violence of her dream alarmed me, but I stayed in her arms until the jolting subsided.

In the morning my fever was gone and my throat better, but I felt disconnected from my surroundings. Ray recalled nothing of the nightmare that had assailed her during the night, but she too seemed remote. I had retreated deep inside and could do nothing to diminish her obvious distance. The three of us went to breakfast at the diner. Ray looked at the menu with distaste but ordered an English muffin. Her face looked as if she'd scraped a dull razor across it.

Edith asked for coffee and poached eggs and said to me, "You have to eat something." She gave the waitress an exasperated look and said, "Bring her coffee, orange juice, and whole wheat toast, please."

I nibbled the bread and gazed out the window at fog that seemed to thicken by the minute. Edith pulled out her phone and called Mrs. Montoya. I was dimly aware of Ray sitting next to me like someone with whom I was barely acquainted.

She hadn't spoken a word since ordering. I placed my hand on her arm and she turned to me with a blank look.

"You okay?" I asked.

Ray moved her stranger's gaze from me and stared straight ahead past Edith as she got off the phone.

"She'll meet us there," Edith said. "At the street end of the drive."

We paid and started out to the cars, the crunch of shoes on gravel far off in my ears, my legs like marionette limbs controlled by a deficient puppeteer. Ray went on ahead. Edith tapped my arm and stopped to face me. In the graying fog she took my hands. Her touch drew my focus so that she appeared the only real and solid thing in the deepening haze. I pulled back in a spasm of apprehension as I imagined the fog to be smoke and Edith a manifestation.

She held tight to my hands and the moment passed. She was Aunt Edith again, the delicate thread of her Shalimar reassuring.

"Beth." She waited until I met her eyes. "I understand what you're going through. I told you and Ray the things I know, but I didn't tell you everything. Later I will, when you're both stronger. But she didn't ask again last night, and I wasn't about to say. It has to do with my husband. Ray's uncle."

I gave her a curious look.

Edith pressed my hands together. "Don't become the third kind of ghost."

My eyes stayed on her face.

"A casualty of the fight against them. You did what you had to. You saved Ray's life. Jack was already dead when I got to him."

She dropped my hands and walked away, the barn coat

loose and crooked on her small frame. I watched her and felt myself fighting not to dissolve into the fog.

It was the thought of Ray that hauled me through.

"Make sure you drive," Edith called to me.

Ray was in the passenger seat of our car.

"Talk to me," I said pulling out after Edith onto the road. "Try to remember your nightmare from last night."

"I'd rather not," she said quietly.

I put aside my disquiet and focused on tailing Edith's sedan through the fog. For a few moments the world around me tunneled to encompass nothing but the murk blanketing the windshield. In my head I saw us on a sheet of snowy ice, me gunning the accelerator to catch up with Edith's car, the engine roaring its approval of my exhilaration until the car ahead stopped and I slammed the brakes, spinning us right into its rear.

I lurched out of the vision and saw Edith's taillights about ten feet ahead. We were near the house.

At the end of the driveway I turned off the engine and we sat in silence as Edith and Mrs. Montoya, a large woman wearing a leopard hat, greeted one another and conferred by Edith's car.

One catastrophic moment. For all I knew, Edith was insane and I had killed a human child.

Except I didn't believe that.

There would be other catastrophic moments. It was never just one.

I looked at Ray. She was already looking at me. "I heard what she said to you about the third kind of ghost."

"You did? You were so far ahead."

"Not really. I heard everything." She opened the door. "I'm ready now."

"You are?"

"Are you?" She stepped out without waiting for me to reply.

I took a deep breath and let it sit in my lungs a while. Then I pulled the keys out of the ignition and followed her.

# CRADLE SONG

## Brenda Kalt

I have published eight stories, including two reprints. My career includes stints as a technical writer and as a software tester. I live in central North Carolina with my husband and cat.

Alone in the ballroom, Evaline Jacobsen wrestled the sprayer from her arms onto the housekeeping cart. Although the governor's palace had absorbed the old baby hospital decades before, every renovation seemed to leave a crack around some tall window. Sealing the edges of the windows meant that none of the sulfur-laden Pallarene atmosphere would spoil the governor's last evening in office.

Behind her a door opened and closed. "A few more minutes. Eight o'clock," she called. Footsteps sounded through the ballroom, and she turned to see the intruder. And stared.

The guest of honor, Governor Paul D'Avanzi himself, was striding toward Evaline. "I'm leaving now. I'll call a shuttle." He dumped a black robe into her arms and held up a cylinder the size of two fingers. "Say your name."

Evaline blinked. "I'm Evaline Jacobsen."

He pressed a spot on the cylinder and handed it to Evaline. "This is a video of my speech. Give it to the emcee yourself. Your voice just authenticated it." He turned away.

As she slid the recorder in among the bottles, Evaline realized that the man was abandoning his own farewell party. She hurried after him. "Governor, you can't leave now. I cleaned everything." She shoved the robe at him, and it fell to the floor.

"I'm sorry." She stooped to retrieve it and saw that the governor's left hand and wrist were purple. "What happened to your hand? Can I call a doctor?"

"No. It's a prosthesis."

Evaline looked up at him.

"It's artificial. When the motor shorted out this afternoon, the pigment sank to the lowest place." He pushed up his sleeve to reveal the line where purple met dead white. "I've kept quiet about it for the last three years, and I don't intend to tell the people of Pallarus the night before I go."

"Nobody wants to lose an arm or a leg," Evaline said. She folded the robe over her arm. "It's nothing to be ashamed of."

He laughed harshly. "I didn't *lose* it, I know exactly where it is. It's in a trash pit beside Lake Yana on Novy Norilsk."

"I never heard of that."

"It's where stupid rich boys go to race iceboats. I crashed during a race and broke my arm in four places. I told the medic to amputate, and I'd get it fixed when I got home." He put a sneer into the word.

Evaline frowned. After a second she asked, "Why didn't you?"

D'Avanzi glared at her. "Because I'm allergic to regenerants. Because the doctors stuffed my host mother with immunosuppressants. Because my host mother and I were a bad match. Because my parents went on the black market because no D'Avanzi would admit to fertility problems." He shook his head. "Because my parents didn't tell me any of this."

"Oh." Evaline stood still. "How did they know about the bad match?"

He sighed. "The host mother got four of my parents' embryos before me. They implanted and vanished. Or they never implanted. But I was the last one, and if the hospital wanted to get paid, they had to produce a baby. Whatever it took."

"Cara was okay, then. She was the only embryo they gave me."

He looked at her. "*You* were a host mother?"

Evaline nodded. "I was. Right here in the baby hospital."

He frowned. "But host mothers forget about their babies. They get all kinds of injections."

"I didn't. The parents didn't show up when I delivered, and the police kept questioning me about whether the baby was hosted or mine. Finally it was too late to start the shots, and there was still no one to take the baby. So I kept her." She wrapped her arms around herself and pressed her hand to her mouth for a moment. "I named her Cara. My dear one. We lived in my flat, and I bought her lots of little dresses and things. I was going to take her home to Innerhaven." Her voice constricted to a whisper. "Three weeks before the year was up the parents came."

"Good God." He stared at Evaline. "Where had they been?"

"They had separated, on different planets, and then they got back together."

"Why didn't you fight?"

"I went to see a lawyer, but he said all I could do was delay and hope. I didn't have that kind of money."

D'Avanzi was silent.

Evaline wiped her nose and stuck the tissue in the trash bag on the cart. She looked away. "Cara had been so good that day. She'd been happy and giggling and trying to walk." She shook her head. "I couldn't have her feel my misery and then lose me. I called the parents from the lawyer's office, and half an hour later they were downstairs." She took a deep breath.

"Cara was asleep, so I just kissed her. I went out before they came in. I didn't want to see them with her."

The clock struck the first chime. Evaline jumped and looked down at the robe in her arms. She shook it out. "Governor, it's time. Put your left hand in your pocket and no one will see it." She pulled the sleeve over his limp arm and stretched the robe around his shoulders.

D'Avanzi did not move.

Evaline said, "Your host mother would have done anything to fix your immune system, if she could have."

He smiled slightly and looked down at Evaline. "So host mothers love their children? For a little while, anyway?"

Evaline tucked the cold hand into the pocket and draped the sleeve over it. "I do, Governor. I love her every day."

# SALT-SKIN AND PIE

## Alena Sullivan

Alena Sullivan, 24, holds
a degree in Cultural
Anthropology and works as
a nanny for two wonderful
human children. She lives in an
apartment-gone-witch-cottage
in Decatur, Georgia, with three
birds and a cat, all of which still
refuse to help her get dressed
in the morning.

Alena works as a fiction writer,
poet, and visual artist, focusing
on identity within narrative and
the repeated cultural pattern
formed by fairy and folk tales.
Her work can be found in
Luna Station Quarterly, Urban
Fantasy Magazine, Goblin
Fruit, Illumen, the Wormwood
Press, and Expanded Horizons
Magazine.

I find it right where I left it, wrapped in an old sheet under a loose floorboard. I remember, a decade ago, wondering if people really hid things that way and searching the whole house for a place where he hadn't sealed everything perfectly. I couldn't find one—he always paid such attention to detail; I'd had to wiggle it loose myself and pry it up to fit anything beneath it.

My hiding spot is just under the window that looks out over the garden, and the clean smell of lavender and rosemary is immediately overwhelmed by the sharp smell of salt as I peel away the sheet. Salt has dried in the creases of the sealskin, white crystals now, and it falls, clattering, to the floor as I shake out the skin. It smells like something else, too, something deeper and darker than salt, something cold and silent and soft. I swallow hard against the urge to cry and refold the skin with shaking hands, tucking it into the wide reed basket I usually use when I go to the market. It's too big, shapeless grey wrinkles spilling over the edges of the basket, making the whole thing look haphazardly done despite my care.

My whole life here might as well be just the same.

There are still two mugs on the table, one wide-based and wide-mouthed with a narrow waist, the whole thing glazed a delicate green-blue (Sean's), and one round and fat-bellied, with a pattern of yellow flowers on white clay (mine). My cup is empty; I've had a dozen cups of tea since. His is still half full, milk going slowly sour even in the cold November air.

I put the kettle on again. I have all the time in the world now; I can make another cup of tea.

I settle at the table, basket in front of me, fingers absently tracing the muted grey folds of the skin inside it. I remember getting out of bed that first night, stumbling but silent, desperate to hide it where he couldn't find it and steal it from me. I had heard the stories.

Weeks later, I had been just as glad to have hidden it—not because he would've stolen it, he wouldn't, he would never—but because if he'd known what I was, known what I was setting aside to make a life here, with him, he would've shoved the skin into my arms and me out the door with it, certain he wasn't worth giving up anything at all.

Eyeing the congealed tea in his mug, I wonder.

Turning my eye on the skin—and it does feel like the skin, not like my skin, now, after more than ten years—I wonder, too, if there is anything for me if I slip it on again. I have this irrational notion that if I disappear into the water, I will do just that—simply disappear. The world I created with him feels real, concrete and warm and comfortable. Everything before that is a haze of deep, deep blue and the bone-humming cold of the sea.

The kettle whistles. I add another bag to the teapot, not bothering to clear out the four already wetly lumped into the bottom.

The steam burns me a little when I pour the water into the teapot, and I feel as though it's cleaning me, a little. As though, in one small spot on my inner wrist, the skin is made new, untouched by sea and man. It's ridiculous, I know, but I feel a little hysterical.

By the time I twitch myself back into the present moment, the tea has steeped enough to pour. My hand shakes a little, but I lift the teapot—a mundane sort of a thing, ceramic patterned with loose interpretations of red and yellow flowers, utilitarian and heavy—and pour the tea into my mug, erasing the tea rings in the bottom of it with the influx of near-boiling liquid. It's probably not especially sanitary, but I can't quite bring myself to care. Next, a spoonful of honey from McKenna's bees and a dollop of cream from O'Leary's cows, then a quick stir to blend it all together. My hand shakes a little too hard, and a splash of tea goes over the side of the mug, obscuring one of the little yellow flowers and trickling down to form a ring around the cup's base. It smudges when I lift the cup, hands still shaking a little, and take a too-hot sip so it doesn't spill again.

It tastes like the life I've built here, like the family of neighbors who've gifted us with things like honey and cream, like every single morning I've woken to find blue eyes staring into my own.

You have such beautiful eyes, he'd say, every morning without fail.

They aren't even really a color, I'd argue, smiling despite myself.

Black as sloe, he'd quip back, bumping his nose against mine and grinning at me, and bright as stars on water.

It was the sort of poetic thing that men say to women to make them swoon, but he was never poetic about anything else, really, Sean was far too practical a man for that, so I believed him then. I still do, despite the fact that I woke up alone these last mornings. I don't think he left because he didn't love me.

That would be better, somehow, I think. Cleaner. I could stand, I think, being unloved. It's the idea that he loved me and still thought he could make the choice for me, over my head, that I was better without him—it rankles. As though I weren't strong, weren't something ancient and capable of surviving the coldest and the darkest places, of gliding, soundless and smooth, through worlds he couldn't begin to imagine.

Then again, he never knew, so perhaps that part is my fault.

I drink the better part of the cup of tea, letting it burn my mouth a little—unlike the steam, it doesn't feel like it's cleansing me, really, and I can't stand that my mouth still tastes like kissing him. It's been two days and dozens of cups of tea; you'd think I'd taste sleep and bitter leaves, not—not him kissing me carefully, like he was making sure it was precisely perfect, and saying, while I was still too asleep to understand, much less argue,

I love you, you've done nothing wrong, but I ruin everything I touch and I can't do it to you, too.

When I woke, hours later, and found the house empty of his things, I understood, but it was a sour sort of comprehension. Losing the child was no one's fault—mine, if anything, not his—but he's never been good at being kind to himself. His parents were never kind, blaming him for everything, and he took up that work for them when he was grown.

Gently, fingertips hesitant, I smooth my fingers over my belly. It's flatter than it was when I came here, still soft from the water, and far flatter than it should be, more than four months after conceiving. I'd lost the child just a week ago, after a bad fall on the path down to the water, bringing Sean his forgotten lunch before he went out on the boat. I got nervous, every time, going down by the sea—in this skin, I'm so fragile, and I know exactly how quickly the water can kill these soft, pink people, too thin and too quickly drowned or frozen. I'd been paying more attention to the water than to my feet, and I'd slipped, a loose stone shifting under my foot, and—

And that had been that.

Sean kept saying it was his fault for forgetting to bring his lunch himself. It's nonsense, really—I could've fallen doing anything, distracted as I was by the sound of the water. I don't even know that it's my fault; I don't know that these things have fault; they just are. Maybe that's the wild creature in me, the predator who has devoured the young of others without a thought. But it doesn't feel like there's fault, and certainly not his.

I press my palm, hard, into the thin flesh of my belly, and I realize, a little dimly and with some disappointment, that I can't leave today. I'm too thin now, and even in a sealskin, I'll freeze in minutes. I'll drown. I can bear the uncertainty of putting the skin back on, of not knowing if the magic's still there, if I still have the sea in my blood at all—I can manage the possibility of death, but, even as much as my heart hurts now, I can't bear the certainty of it.

Letting my mug bang a little harder than necessary against the table as I put it down, I pick up the sealskin from the basket and tuck it in a folded heap into the chair next to mine. It will have to wait. For now—I look around the kitchen, already knowing what I'll find. A heel of bread on the counter, stale, destined for O'Leary's chickens, and an apple in the bowl on the table. Certainly not enough to put on the sort of fat I'd need to survive the water in November.

Humming tunelessly, the sound of water rushing in my head, I put the basket—now smelling strongly of salt—over my arm, and gathering my shawl around my shoulders, head out the door and to the market.

\*\*\*

"Five pies?" Mrs. O'Neal repeats, one eyebrow sharply arched.

"Five pies," I agree steadily. "Three fish, I don't mind the kind, one lamb, one potato and veg."

"You feeding an army now, are you, Mrs. Delaney?" she asks, not budging a bit, certainly not going off to put together my order.

I flinch a bit at the name. I took the ring off last night, left it on the nightstand, the gold gleaming and out of place on the wood. My hand feels naked and vulnerable without it, but that feels right, in its own harsh sort of way. Even without it, though, the town knows me. There's no escaping the name I've gone by for ten years. "Not an army, just myself," I say, forcing a thin smile. Just myself, indeed.

"You've ordered two pies a week for six years, and never more. I know you're having a hard time, with your man walking out, but there's no call to let yourself go." She pats my hand kindly, face full of pity, and I wonder if the whole town knows already. Probably. There's few enough folk here.

"I'm just stocking up for the week," I lie. "I—"

"Just give the woman her pies, Maura, for Christ's sakes," Mr. O'Neal snaps, rolling his eyes and elbowing his wife none too gently.

Mrs. O'Neal pulls a face. "Language, John. I'm just worried for the lass's health, you know, she's ordering five pies, and she's only ever—"

Mr. O'Neal rolls his eyes again. "Then more coin for us, woman, my god. Here, Mrs. Delaney, and take a sixth at half price if you like it." He begins wrapping and stacking the pies without waiting for his wife to say anything, and she just crosses her arms and huffs.

Feeling a little contrary, I say, "I'd love that, Mr. O'Neal, and thank you."

"Another lamb, maybe?" he offers, and it's brusque and businesslike and feels a world kinder than Mrs. O'Neal's sympathy.

"That'd be lovely," I agree. Lamb is quite fatty, even if I prefer the taste of fish. The taste isn't really the point.

Mr. O'Neal smiles at me as he transfers the pies into my basket. "Excellent, excellent. That'll be seventeen and fifty."

I hand over the money without hesitating, smiling without looking him in the eye, and wonder where I'll have to go to get my pies tomorrow. Even Mr. O'Neal will start to wonder at me putting away six pies a day.

I make my way to the produce stall next, mostly because I can feel Mrs. O'Neal's eyes still on me, and I don't want to head straight for the sweets with her watching. Contrary as I might feel, I don't really want the whole town sheltering me from eating too much, and I fully believe Mrs. O'Neal capable of convincing at least half of them that they ought to be managing me.

I really do hate being managed. Sean's leaving feels remarkably like being managed, done for my benefit, in his head, and I feel sick when I think of it. Any shadow of the same feeling is better avoided.

"Anything I can get for you, Mrs. Delaney?" Mr. Ashe asks kindly—too kindly, really, and I know he knows, too.

Smiling what I suspect is a terrible rictus of a smile, I try to come up with something that will actually do me some good. Apples with cheese, maybe, for when I can't stand another pie. "Apples, please."

"Apples, apples," he agrees, waving a hand at the display. "Red or green?"

I've only eaten green apples for years; Sean didn't like the red. "Red," I say, decisively, "a half-dozen, please."

He bobs his head—Mr. Ashe is always bouncing a bit, a thin beanpole of a man always on the move, like the wind is blowing him this way and that—and tucks the apples into my basket carefully, nestling them between the wrapped pies and the basket's edge so they don't bruise. "Mrs. Delaney," he says, carefully, like he's sorry to be saying anything personal at all, "please allow me to extend—"

"I rather wish you wouldn't," I say, a little sharper than I mean to.

He doesn't balk, though, doesn't flinch at all, just nods. "Take the apples, then, and don't mind the cost."

"I couldn't," I protest, appreciating this practical approach to kindness but not wanting to accept the sympathy, either.

He smiles, a lopsided sort of thing, and doesn't look at me when he says, "My Jeannie left me going on six years ago. I didn't want anyone's pity, either, but I damn well could've used any useful sort of kindness. Take the apples, Mrs. Delaney, and not a word about it." He nods again, firmly, decisively, handing back my basket and turning away immediately so I can't argue any further.

I smile, almost a real one, and dip my head in thanks. I can't actually make myself say the words, but I'm grateful nonetheless.

Mrs. O'Neal is minding her own business for the moment, so I turn for the sweets stall and collect as many fattening treats as I think I can manage without Mrs. Sheehy giving me the eye.

*** 

I can't bear eating at the kitchen table. It's too lonely with Sean's chair empty. It's the same problem with the bed—I've had to take my pillow and the quilt down to the floor, despite the cold, to sleep at all. To eat, I take two pies to the windowsill and begin to eat standing up, looking out at the path down to the sea. It's rocky and bare at this time of year, the gorse bushes brown and sharp with needles, none of the yellow flowers to be found, and I can see the line of the beach where Sean's boat is usually moored. The deep groove it leaves in the sand is gone, washed away with the first high tide, all signs of him gone. I wonder where he's gone, if it's far—it must be, he wouldn't want to leave any chance that I'd find him if I broke down and lost all sense of shame and went to look for him. It's not shame that keeps me from looking, though—I wouldn't have any, I think, really—but a certainty that it wouldn't do any good, and would hurt us both twice over.

I can see the spot where I fell, and lost Sean as well as the baby: a sharp twist in the path as it curves through the rocks and down to the beach. There's no mark there, but it feels like there should be, some bloody stain on the sand to mark all the things that I'd given up to come here, to live this life, and then all remains of this life, too.

I've set aside my pie before I've really thought of it, making my way outside with a quick stop to the nightstand on the way. The ring is cool in my hand, unwarmed by skin for two days now. It nestles neatly into the sandy soil by the side of the path at that curve where I fell, sinking in with just a gentle push of my fingers.

I can't lift big rocks, but I gather as many small ones as I can find and begin to build a little cairn over it, hiding the gold circle with grey stone. The stones are rough and scrape my hands a little, reddening my palms. I'm careless as I go, wind whipping my hair into a black cloud that covers my face and whips away any tears I might be crying—I am, I know I am, but it's much easier to pretend I'm not—and there's a spot or two of blood from my hands smudged into the stone by the time I'm done. It feels right that there's some of it left there, even if the rain will wash it out. All traces of me, swept away by water, like the groove of Sean's boat in the sand. Self-indulgent, maybe, but symmetrical.

I spend too long there, on my knees by the little cairn, no thoughts that have words in my head at all, praying by way of offering up my own emptiness to whatever gods might use it, and by the time I make my way back to the house, my pies are cold.

***

As I'm making my way to Mrs. O'Neal's the next day, a hand slips into the crook of my elbow and tugs me off the road, into the shadow between two stalls.

I'd be worried about having my purse stolen, but the woman is small, elfish and pale, and I think I could probably knock her out cold if need be. She's not familiar to me, her face thin and freckled, and while she's small, she's easily more than twenty.

"Can I help you?" I ask, when she says nothing at all, her hand still on my elbow.

She snaps out of it then, face coloring, and she says, "Pies."

"I don't have any yet," I say apologetically, thinking she's asking for a handout. She's thin enough to need it. I'm nervous about trying to go back to the O'Neals' stall again—if the order yesterday made Mrs. O'Neal balk, doing it two days in a row is sure to raise questions. I doubt she'd take I'm fattening up so I don't freeze to death when I put on my sealskin and go back to the sea as an explanation. She'd probably just take it as an excuse to try to sell me on one of her diets. Maybe I can convince her that eating loads of pies is a diet.

"No, no," she says, shaking her head, "sorry, I—I meant, I have pies, if you'd like to buy them."

My eyebrows come together at that. "You aren't a merchant here."

She shakes her head. "No, no, I've just—I've just come to live with my aunt, and she's old, she's—she's quite old, and I'm meant to be bringing in money, but no one here will hire me, since they don't know me yet, and—" She stops, hands waving a little in explanation. Her accent is foreign, vowels thick and heavy, and she seems at a loss for words.

"I see," I assure her, smiling a little. She's a nervous sort, stammering here and there in her rush to get her words out, and I remember that feeling. The desperation for these people to like me, to count me as one of their own. "Where are you from?"

She goes paler, if that's possible, and shakes her head. She's backing away as she says, "Never mind, I'll leave you to it, I'm sorry to bother you, miss—"

It's the fact that she doesn't know my name that makes me put my hand out to stop her. "What kind of pies do you have?" I remember the panic that had set in when people asked me where I was from, what my name was. I had no name until Sean gave me his—even now, I have only been Mrs. Delaney to these people, and Mavourneen, mo mhuírnín, to Sean, at home. My darling. It's not really a name, even, not one I can tell folk to call me out in the world.

She breaks out in a full grin. "Any kind you like. I've a couple lamb ones made, but I can make up any sort you want, as many—I saw you, yesterday? With the baker's wife, and her not wanting to—it's none of my business, and I would be grateful for it."

Falling rather desperately in love with the idea of not having to argue with Mrs. O'Neal every day for the next few weeks, I ask, "Do you think I could get five or six a day, then?"

She nods, not even hesitating, hands wringing at her apron a bit, but no judgment on her face. She's sort of tucked into herself, shy or frightened and forced into interaction by necessity, but warmed to conversation by the prospect of business. "I can do that, no problem at all. Do you mind what kind?"

"Something fattening," I say baldly, testing the waters, making sure she's not going to balk.

"Loads of butter it is, then," she agrees, grin widening, eyes crinkling. They're green as sea glass, catching the light, and I think she might be beautiful if she weren't so scared of whatever made her start to run when I started to question her. "Lamb, maybe, and beef, if I can get it, and fish with cream sauce when I can't."

"How much for six today, then?"

"Fifteen," she says easily, and it's too low, really, but I know she's undercharging because she's not meant to be doing business here.

"Eighteen," I counter. I've nothing to save for, now, really—I won't need the money where I'm going.

She huffs a laugh. "Maybe tomorrow. Make sure you like them, first."

I feel a grin start to spread across my own face, despite the hollow feeling that's been living under my breastbone these past days. "As you like it," I agree, trying to put the smile back where it came from with no luck.

She leads me back to her aunt's house—though there's no one else in evidence—a ramshackle sort of cottage made of whitewashed stone and set with a red door. The wood is warped, a bit, and the roof has clearly seen better days, but there are pots of flowers under the windows, and it's a cheerful sort of place.

"Just wait a bit while I make up the others, yeah?" she says, gesturing to the small table in the kitchen as we go inside, already heading for the kitchen. "I've the pastry made up, they'll just take a little to bake up." Her speech follows the local patterns well enough, but her vowels are still strange, unfamiliarly set.

I settle at the table without a word, setting my empty basket at my feet. It still gives off a smell of salt, as though I left it soaking in the ocean for days.

"Don't mind the cat," the woman adds, already elbow-deep in pie effluvia. She's quick with her movements, efficient. "She's a stray or something, comes begging in for scraps." Her words are offhand, but there's something to her tone that says she's secretly fond of the thing. She's a stray of her own sort, though, for sure—we both are, at that, and I look around for the cat.

It's a ragged little tabby, tail too short, like it's been bitten off by something. She's hovering in the doorway, hesitant, sniffing at the air. "Hello, you," I say to her, putting my fingers out for her to examine.

She trots closer, sniffing at each of my fingers in turn and then butting her head against my hand when she finds them satisfactory. They probably smell of pies and cheese, with how much I've been eating. She purrs softly as I rub a hand over the back of her head and behind her ears.

"Here," the woman says, handing me a small wedge of stale-looking cheese with fingers smudged with flour. "If she starts begging at you."

I break off a chunk of the cheese and offer it to the cat, heading off the begging before it begins. No woman should have to beg for kindness, even if she's a cat.

When I look up, the woman is smiling at me approvingly. "I'm Nora," she says, clearly lying, the name obviously unfamiliar on her tongue, but also trying to offer something of herself, to connect.

I don't push it, because I have no name to offer in return. I feed another chunk of cheese to the cat. "Well met," I say, eventually, because she's clearly waiting for a response.

She laughs a little, under her breath, and returns to the pies. "Well met, indeed."

***

Nora's pies are better than the O'Neals'. I feel a bit blasphemous thinking it, given how many years I've been buying from the O'Neals, but Nora's are rich with butter, and she doesn't hesitate with spices. She's from somewhere far away, then, some city where Eastern spices are easier to come by, because there's paprika and turmeric in some of them, just little pinches, but the flavor is worlds away from the local fare. Starved as I am for the unfamiliar, for things that don't feel like the decade of patterns with Sean, I devour them. I stand at the window, looking at the little cairn mourning the life I chose, and I eat them, one after the other, and hum the tuneless song of light filtering through water.

The fat is slow to come, but builds quickly once it's started. Over the weeks, my face grows rounder, pushing out the lines carved by years of smiling, making it smooth and moon-shaped. My belly and hips grow fuller, my bosom deepening, my fingers growing fat. It feels more like my real skin than the seal flesh waiting on my kitchen chair, even—I recognize my own face, now, apple-cheeked and dark-eyed, when I catch sight of my reflection. Mrs. O'Neal gives me pitying looks when I pass her stall in the market, but I let myself go years ago, lost in the full feeling of love, forgetting to eat and doing my best to keep the figure in fashion among the women of the town. I wonder, if I'd been well-fed and softer, if maybe I wouldn't have lost the baby so easily. I won't ever know—there is no life for me here without Sean, nothing to make me stay and try to find another man, even for the sake of having a child to love. I will not find a lover among my own kind, either, I know.

I mourn the thought of future children more than I thought I could. Not the baby I lost—that was an accident of life, unavoidable—but the idea of the chance to try again, to have a child with my black curls and Sean's blue eyes, laughing up at me with a face shaped by both of ours. The thought of that child never walking in the world at all guts me.

I eat another pie to fill the aching hole in my belly, and relish the way the layer of protective fat grows. There is no shame in this softness, whatever Mrs. O'Neal and the women of the town might think, regardless of what's in fashion. This softness is safety, is protection from the harshness of the world, and even if I weren't building it up for the sake of going back to my home, my people, I think I would be pleased with it anyway.

I lick my fingers clean, tasting paprika and turmeric and the work of another woman who has chosen to lose herself for a new life. I spend time imagining what her real name might be, rather than what my child would have looked like, because it hurts much less, and there is a chance of knowing one of those things, if not the other.

*** 

"I think she needs a name," Nora says to me one day, gesturing with a large wooden spoon at the tabby curled up in my lap. The cat twitches an ear, to inform us that she's listening, but doesn't otherwise deign to move.

"Don't we all," I mutter under my breath, feeling a wry smile tugging at the edge of my mouth.

Nora cracks a smile of her own and sets down her spoon, hugging herself a little. She does that often, like she's hiding something broken in her middle that she doesn't want anyone to see. It's a familiar gesture. I wonder what's been taken from her, what sent her here. "Not anything silly, you know, like people generally give to cats. Not Whiskers or Boots or anything." She leans against the counter, letting the pies finish up in the oven and considering the cat with a critical eye.

"No," I agree, stroking careful fingers over the cat's head, "she deserves something dignified." We're too often stripped of our dignity, I think, women.

"Jeannie, maybe," Nora muses.

"Everyone here is named Jeannie," I counter, laughing a little. "There's Young Jeannie and Jeannie Mac, and then Jeannie O'Leary, the fourth daughter of the O'Learys, and the Jeannie who was married to Mr. Ashe but ran off, and—"

"So not Jeannie, then," Nora cuts in, laughing properly. "What's your idea, then, miss knows-everything?"

I have no idea how to go about naming things. I was never even able to name myself. "I don't—"

"Fiona, then? Kathleen?" she tries, watching the cat for any sort of response. The tabby yawns, unimpressed. "Coleen, Mara, Aoife, Jenny—"

The cat's ear twitches, just a little, and I nod. "Jenny it is," I say, rubbing the ear between my fingers. She purrs a little louder, assenting, and Nora snorts.

"Bit of a common name, Jenny," Nora says teasingly.

"Plenty dignified for a cat, though, I think," I say, and it feels, for the first time in weeks, like I'm conversing normally, just a woman talking about day-to-day things with someone, easily, without choosing every word like it's a sharp thing, handled with care. I could miss this, maybe, and that feels terrifying in its own right, but I savor it, anyway. I can still leave even if I have something small to miss.

"Right, then," Nora says, all business again, as though she noticed the easiness and found it odd, too. She wipes her hands needlessly on her apron and gets the pot holders, pulling the pies from the oven. They smell magnificent—mostly fish today, stuffed full of a heavy cream sauce and vegetables as well—and I breathe deeply, letting my eyes drift shut.

Under the rich smell of pies, I can still smell the salt in my basket, and it jerks me back to the moment, sharp and real, reminding me of home and the fact that absolutely no one is waiting there for me.

"I should go," I say, swallowing against the lump in my throat. The cat—Jenny—feeling my tension, jumps lightly off my lap and begins to twine around my ankles.

"Right," Nora agrees, nodding her head, gesturing at the pies, "just, ah—just give them a minute to cool off and I'll wrap them right up for you."

I wait, feeling tightly wound, for what feels like years, until Nora breaks and starts wrapping the pies, brown paper crinkling. "You could—I mean, if you wanted to, you could stay to eat. Sometime, I mean." She's facing away from me, head down over the pies, shoulders drawn up tightly, like she's as nervous making the offer as I am with the idea of accepting it.

"Thank you," I say, because I know she doesn't know what's happened in my life, isn't offering out of pity, so the offer feels genuine, feels clean. I haven't seen her aunt even once, and I suspect she's lonely, and, well, I've been something uglier than lonely for weeks now. "I—I might like that, sometime, maybe."

Her shoulders relax a little, and when she turns to beam at me, she's beautiful. There are lines around her mouth, and I think they're from hurt rather than smiling overmuch, but her eyes crinkle up and sparkle a bright green, and the freckles beneath them make her look younger and hopeful. "Any time," she says, utterly sincere. "Tomorrow, even."

"All right," I agree, meaning it. "Tomorrow."

***

I'm nearly fat enough, now. My belly hangs out over my hips, soft and round and yielding to my hand when I smooth a palm over it. I've had to let my dresses out. I can leave in a week or two, I think, when the weather warms up.

I spread the sealskin out on the bed, now empty of linens and pillows—they're all huddled in the corner of the kitchen, by the stove, where I've taken to sleeping, a sort of messy little nest for myself. Somehow, there's still more salt in it, and it makes a soft clattering as it spills to the floor.

I step back, admiring the smooth greyness of the skin, little pebbles of salt crunching under my bare feet. I have had feet for a long time. It will be strange to lose them.

The kettle whistles. Leaving the sealskin where I've laid it, I put a fresh bag in the teapot—on its own, this time; I've cleaned out the soggy stack of its predecessors—and pour the water over it. I think I'll leave a note that Nora may have my things when I'm gone, if she'd like them. Such a sturdy teapot would do her delicate hands good, and the things I've collected in my time here deserve to be loved.

I remember buying this teapot with Sean, remember choosing carefully between the row of them with different colored flowers decorating their bellies. I remember loving my mug when he brought it home for me, marveling at the little gorse flowers in their elegant abstractions. I remember making the quilt that I've spent the last five and a half years sleeping under out of our old clothes when they wore too thin to wear any longer. I don't love any of the things on their own, though—the gorse flowers are too garish a yellow, the teapot too sunny in its colors, the quilt too bare and ragged. It was the warmth of the space between us that I loved, that brought me out of the water in the first place. When he looked at me, I'd felt flooded with sunlight, like he couldn't imagine anything better than me in all the world.

I've started to look again like I did then, rounded and soft, smooth and fat as a river stone. I wonder if he'd look at me like he did that first time, if he saw me again, or if his human need to feel broken and guilty would outweigh whatever charms I had, even back then. I don't think the man he's become would even know how to fall in love. In the beginning, the way he hurt was like a beacon to me—I think it is for many women, human and other alike; we have this call to nurture, to heal and soothe. We all want to be needed, I think. I didn't think I could fix him, of course not, but that was because, of the two of us, I was the only one who didn't think he was broken. Perhaps I was wrong. I do not know if an unbroken man can leave a woman he loves while she still loves him.

I wonder if he thought I could fix him. If my strangeness was a balm to him, the promise of some magical cure for whatever hurt in his heart. I hope not; no one can live up to such a thing, and if that was what was in his mind, I hate to have offered him any false hope.

I wonder if my heart is broken.

I rub a hand over the soft flesh shielding my breastbone and feel the ache beneath it. The hurt there is jagged, brittle and dangerous, but I don't think I am broken. Perhaps the thicket of humanity I have grown in these long years is cut away, bleeding sap and trailing brambles, but I think the core of me is too inhuman to be broken. I wish otherwise, a little—I think there would be something cathartic and awfully beautiful in breaking entirely, in falling to the ground to weep and wither.

I pour the tea into my round little gorse mug and mix in the cream and honey. It has begun to taste foreign to me again, as it did when I first stumbled through the doorway on new, awkward legs. Sean had sat me down, poured me tea in his blue-green mug, and wrapped my hands around it to keep them warm. As if I would be cold, this close to the sun.

Almost involuntarily, I mimic the gesture now—the fingers of one hand overlapping those of the other, the warm clay cradled between my palms.

It is not the same, I think, to comfort yourself as it is to be offered comfort.

\*\*\*

"I've made—I've made us something other than pies, if that's alright," Nora says, nervous again for the first time in weeks. She's rubbing her hands shakily over her arms, hugging herself a little. "I mean, I've your pies here, set aside for you to take with you, but—I mean, if you're still wanting to eat here—"

I laugh a little, I can't help it, as I settle at the table and gather Jenny into my lap, fingers rubbing carefully under her chin, waiting for the purr before I begin to stroke my hand across her back. "What are we having?"

Nora relaxes a little. "Goulash. It's a sort of stew that we make where I come from," she says carefully, shoulders still pulled up high to her neck. It's the most she's given away about herself in the weeks I've known her, much more of an offering than her fake name or the food she's making. "There's meat and onion and vegetables and spices, and—"

My stomach rumbles a little, giving me away, and the tension breaks. "It sounds wonderful," I assure her, shooing the cat off my lap and standing up to help her get the dishes. She makes room for me in the kitchen, and we move around one another with the sort of practical grace of sea birds, one swooping in, the other gliding out, as we gather the dinnerware and set the table. Nora ladles the stew into wooden bowls, laying out slices of boiled egg on dishes beside them, sprinkling them with paprika and salt.

"Mavourneen," I say, quietly, so she can ignore it if she wants to. I feel selfish, taking this offering of her past, her self, without giving anything of my own. This isn't a name, not really—an endearment, if anything, but she isn't from here, probably doesn't even know it's anything other than a name.

Nora smiles, a small, private sort of smile, and repeats it to herself, mouth shaping the sounds carefully. "It's beautiful," she says, as quietly as I said the name, keeping the whole of the conversation in the air between us, secret. She puts a dainty hand on mine and squeezes, as if to reaffirm the unspoken promise of secrecy. "It suits you. Mavourneen."

I ache, then, sharply and deeply, from the middle. It does suit me. I feel wrong, being no one's darling, being naked of affection, of intimacy. This moment, this sharing of this one thing I have kept tucked away, safe and hidden from every-one but him, is like remarrying a world I'd abandoned when Sean left. I feel sick to my stomach, turned over and dropped from a very great height. Hearing that name, that private name, on someone else's tongue makes it real, makes it mine, and the fact that I can't live up to it any longer is a vicious sort of pain.

"I'm sorry," I hear myself saying, numb. I push back from the table, the motion abrupt and sloppy, and the chair screeches on the floor. Jenny jumps back, startled, as I stand on shaky legs. "I'm so sorry," I say again, hands trembling.

I'm out the door before I can look at her. I don't want to see the look on her face.

\*\*\*

The sealskin is heavy across my shoulders, foreign and thick and reeking of salt and a world I left behind a lifetime ago. The wind is high today—March is not a kind month, oncoming Spring or not, and the waves are whipped into frothy white peaks like meringue on top of a churning slate of grey-blue. I make my way down the path on numb feet, slipping here and there and paying no heed.

I pass the cairn without looking at it. I have given too much of myself to this world already, let it carve away at me, let it feed me and clothe me. Let it name me.

I make my way past the naked gorse bushes, feet tripping over stones but pressing forward, the wind shoving me along, as if to say, go, go, do not look back.

The place where Sean moored his boat every day is etched in my mind—it was the place where I first came ashore in this pink skin, first gave up the green and the blue for the smell of peat fires and the taste of apples and potatoes and lamb pies and tea. I find the spot blindly, following the will of my feet, and throw the sealskin down on it.

With shaking hands, I begin to take off my clothes. Coat, apron, dress, petticoats. It's cold, even with the layers of fat I've built up over the last months, and I'm shivering by the time I'm done. I can imagine my people, far out in the water, sleek black heads bobbing among the waves.

Fingers stiff with cold and trembling, I take up the edge of the sealskin. It's still spilling salt everywhere, somehow, pouring little white crystals out onto the sand, and that reassures me, just a little, that the magic hasn't bled from it entirely. Carefully, so carefully, I drape it over me, wrapping it around me like a blanket, leaving my head bare. The tension eases from my shoulders a little as I feel the hum of it recognizing me, clinging to me. Quietly, afraid to give voice to my relief, I sigh.

"This explains more than it doesn't," Nora says with false levity from behind me.

I close my eyes against the smell of baking pies and paprika, swallowing down the unexpected guilt that rises. "Does it?" I ask, to have something to say. Clouds of my dark hair whip across my face, stinging like tears.

"Did he steal it from you, like in the stories they tell here?" she asks. A shaky hand rests on my shoulder, fingers barely pressing down, tracing the line of my shoulder blade under the thick grey of the sealskin.

I choke on a laugh. "Not at all. He used to throw me fish from his boat and tell me stories. I followed him home, and didn't stop when we reached the shore. He never even knew what I was, just thought I was some half-drowned girl who'd hit her head and forgotten where she came from."

Nora's other hand comes to settle on my other shoulder, and they both squeeze, just a little. "It is too cold for this, Mavourneen. Wait for warmer weather."

My darling. I'd meant to. "I can't," I tell her, a little raggedly, a little desperately. "I can't wait at all." If I don't go now, I won't go at all. I can tell.

She sighs, and I feel a shift in her as she steels herself. She wraps her arms around my middle from behind, tucking her chin over my shoulder and squeezing me. I don't know if it's to show affection or to keep me from running into the waves, but it's warm, so I don't pull away. "Solymár, to the East. Eleonóra."

"What?" I ask. The cold is settling in, and my cheeks are burning from the wind.

"Where I'm from, and my name," Nora says gently, like she's talking to an animal that might startle. I suppose she is. "I had—I had a husband there. He was not a good man. I ran away. I do not have an aunt here. I have nothing here; I had to go where he would not look for me, where I had nothing." She squeezes me a little tighter. "I have nothing here but you. Do not go yet."

I shake my head. "I don't even have a name. Not a real one. I am not made for this place. I cannot stay without him. I came here for him, and he is gone." I look out at the water, at the blue-grey sea where my kin are waiting.

"You did not come here for him. You came here for you, to be with him. To be happy. Stay for you, too. Be with yourself, choose to make your own happiness." She huffs a soft laugh, warm on my neck. "Be with me. We will eat too many pies and get very fat and grow old without men, and all the town will whisper and wonder if we are lovers."

"Is that what you want?" I ask, genuinely curious. It had not occurred to me, but the thought is not a frightening or unpleasant one.

She shrugs, and I feel the gesture all along my back, muted by the sealskin. "I do not know, to be honest," she admits. "Love has been only hurt and fear for me, so far. But I know that I want to give you a name. Let them whisper while we decide the rest, yes?"

I consider. The sealskin is growing heavy, buzzing with magic, salt still raining down as the wind ruffles the smooth pelt. "What would you name me, then?" I ask, hearing myself say the words as if from very far away, dim and distant.

Nora hums for a moment. "Gyöngyi," she says, after a moment, or maybe longer. The vowels are strange, and the word sounds like her pies taste—familiar, but not really. "It is my language; I do not know enough of the language here to name you in it properly. Gyöngyi."

I laugh a little, trying to wrap my mouth around the sounds to repeat it, but I do not look away from the sea. "That's quite a mouthful."

She grins against my shoulder. "It means pearl, because you are this shining, round, pale thing from the sea." She presses her palms into the softness of my belly, hugging me tighter. "Do you not like it?"

"I do, actually," I say, feeling the edges of my lips curl into a smile. The wind is not so bitter, now. "You must be cold," I realize, feeling guilty for the first time that she is out here, trying to call me back, at the expense of her own comfort.

"I am," she agrees. "And of the two of us, I am wearing more clothes. Come inside with me, we will have tea and something warm to eat. Little Jenny is guarding the goulash."

I grin at the idea of the spindly tabby standing guard at the stove in that ramshackle little house. I wonder how long it would take to fatten her up, too, her and Nora both, until they are moon-faced and happy. Mrs. O'Neal would be scandalized. "I have tea at the house," I allow, slowly, taking my eyes from the waves, finally, and turning my head enough that I can see her.

She beams at me, green eyes shining. "Tea is good. Warm. We could have tea, then goulash."

"Jenny would miss me, if I left," I try, cautiously, testing out the idea of having something tying me here again.

"Jenny would miss you if you left," Nora agrees. "She would not be the only one," she adds, bumping her forehead against my shoulder.

I breathe a shaky little sigh and let my shoulders drop. The sealskin slips down around them, grey folds pooling around my arms. "The goulash did smell good," I allow, trying to hide a grin. I turn all the way around, turning my back on the sea and the sense of my people. I press my forehead to Nora's, wrapping the edges of the sealskin around her shoulders, too, to share our warmth, burrowing my arms around her middle. "Very good."

Nora laughs, a little hysterical with relief. "It is good," she agrees. "Lots of spices, lots of fat."

"Jenny is too thin," I tell her seriously, not caring that it follows nothing in the conversation at all. "You are, too."

"We are," Nora agrees easily, unbothered. "You will have to help us fix that. Teach us your wise seal-woman ways, Gyöngyi. We will learn."

"You're the only one who knows this, you know," I say, gesturing with my chin at the sealskin.

Nora smiles, her private sort of smile that tells you she has kept bigger secrets than your own and been glad to. "I will tell only Jenny," she promises.

"Good," I say, relaxing into her arms. "Take me home?"

Nora says nothing at all, just takes my hand, twining her long, slim fingers with mine, and gathers my clothes with her other hand. Pressing a kiss to my temple, smile on her mouth, she leads me up the path to the house that was mine, once, and might be again.

My heart only twinges a little, like an old bruise, when we pass the cairn.

# STIFF

## Kellie Coppola

Kellie Coppola grew up in Phoenix, Arizona reading everything she could get her hands on. She is a current MFA student studying fiction at Chapman University. She has previously been published in Phosphene and eleven40seven.

If aliens want to inspect the Earth and take a quick snapshot of mankind, don't send them to New York, London, or LA. Send them to San Francisco at noon. We've got all colors of the rainbow of ethnicity and race, sexual preference and gender, living and dead. Every kind of person you can imagine all trying to find a decent place to eat lunch. Except the Amish, I don't think I've ever seen any Amish people in San Francisco. Maybe the aliens could make a detour to the Midwest.

I didn't always fight the whole of mankind to eat a rushed lunch during the workday. I used to just eat at my desk, taking a break from staring at number columns to stare at news headlines on my computer. But after the edges of my vision started going blurry and an optometrist prescribed me -4.25 lenses, Lisa insisted I leave the office at least an hour a day to give my eyes a rest. Even after she is gone I still find myself wandering out of the office at 12 noon sharp, ever the creature of habit.

I wonder which will be more crowded, the French café on Marigold or the Vietnamese place down near Central?

At the stoplight outside my building I step off the curb when everyone else does, not bothering to check the light. I move with the security of the crowd to the other side and find the wave taking me left. Vietnamese it is.

The crowd carries me thirteen blocks before I muster up some force of will to cut across to another stop walk. The Vietnamese place sits across the street, its red lanterns waving in a slight breeze I can't feel through my suit. A cop stands next to me, waiting on the light, and I feel the strangest urge to grab his gun. I always have this urge whenever I see a cop. It's not that I have violent fantasies; I don't even want to use the gun. I just want to see what would happen next. It's like when you stand on top of a bridge and wonder what it would feel like if you jumped.

The light turns green before I can figure out if today is the day I'll finally act upon this whim and the cop is gone, chasing down some criminals who have parked too long in the metered parking.

I don't know the name of the old woman who works at the front, but she smiles in recognition when I open the door. "Meester Yames, seet anywhere!"

I grab a table for two near the back and pick up the menu, thinking maybe I'll order something new for a change but everything is written in Vietnamese. Instead of asking for an English one, I just give the waitress my usual order. She returns a few minutes later with a bowl of noodles and a smile that I don't know if I return.

A couple next to me expertly feed each other with chopsticks and suddenly I feel self-conscious about slurping through my fork.

"If I wanted to eat with sticks I would go live in the fucking woods like a cavewoman," Lisa used to say loudly. I would turn red at the glares from the Vietnamese servers. They've gotten much nicer since I started coming here without her.

It doesn't take me long to finish the bowl, and by the time

I pay I've only used up twenty minutes of my hour-long break. I'll walk to the park. I do the math. Seven minutes to the park, ten minutes to sit, fifteen back to the office and a two-minute elevator ride should put me back just in time. Another cop stands at the corner and I shove my hands in my pockets as I pass.

I find a bench in the park with difficulty, and now I only have six minutes to relax. The weather has turned nice today; the breeze hits this corner of the city making it an oasis and everyone is out to drink hungrily from the coolness.

A teenager with a Mohawk sits with a Stiff girl across from me. I politely avert my gaze, but somehow every time I find something new to focus on, my eyes drift back to the teenagers. You don't see too many young Stiffs. She's freshly dead; the decomposing process has barely begun. I can still tell that her eyes were a light color, maybe blue or green, but of course they're opaque now, glossed over with a whitish film.

The kid with the Mohawk is reading poetry to her. Something by Shelley. The wind tugs a piece of brown hair from her scalp and sends it down the sidewalk, but neither of them notices.

I wonder what happened to her. Most teenagers are killed by car accidents these days, right? There are no deformities, no missing limbs or gaping wounds like most accident Stiffs have though. Maybe a disease? The wind picks up and I see something flutter at her wrists. Skin. Oh.

The scene reminds me intensely of my mother, and for a minute I'm ten years old again sitting at the table watching her hold a book two inches from her nose. My mother loved to read. Well, she didn't so much read as she breathed in words, like air. She consumed everything, from books to magazines, Hallmark cards and coupons, all those words filling her until I thought she would burst. But she was a quiet woman; she always seemed like she was holding her breath. When I was a child, I would watch my father come up behind her as she read and place his hand on her back. I was sure he was checking to make sure her lungs were still operating.

When my mother died, the words stopped trickling out, but they didn't stop flowing in. She continued to devour everything mechanically, her eyes consuming all the words until they, too, decomposed. Even then, she sat at the kitchen table, staring at books day after day until eventually dad took her to an At Rest home. He had stopped putting his hand on her back.

"He should have done it ages ago, really," Lisa said when I hung up the phone with him. "My grams kept gramps around until there was no motor function left. Made a fucking horrible smell."

An elderly couple walks by and glares at the teenagers. It's not really proper form to take a Stiff out in public but it's becoming more common these days. I don't judge the kid with the Mohawk. How could I when my own father kept my mother around, letting her read for months after she could understand what she was reading?

"Just promise me, when I kick the bucket, you'll put me straight in an At Rest home until I get planted in the ground," Lisa said one night at dinner, after watching a woman with her Stiff husband dining next to us. The woman ate and chatted while the man stared blankly at the flickering flame of the table candle. "Everyone's last memory of me is not going to be some disgusting corpse. They're going to remember me as the beautiful and perfect angel I was in life."

"Angel?"

"You're allowed to embellish when someone's dead. I expect an entire speech about my virtues at my funeral, James Keller."

Of course I promised to follow through on all her wishes, just as she knew I would. I don't consider myself a sentimental person. Even when we signed the divorce papers she left me as her emergency contact because she knew I would put her away, and not dress her up and put her on display the way her mother probably would.

When I leave the park to return to the office the boy in the Mohawk is still reading, and the Stiff girl is still staring at the lamppost, not hearing a word.

Back at the office, the only sounds come from the clicking of computer keys. I take seven silent steps to my seat and sit down. No one looks up or asks me how lunch was. I awaken my computer, and go back to work.

There's something comforting about typing on a keyboard. I barely have to pay attention anymore; I just let my fingers do the work while I think about other things. I used to daydream about Lisa, our plans, our jokes, her smile. Now these long hours are torturous as I try to think about anything else, fail, and then try again while my fingers mechanically punch in long columns of numbers.

Sometimes I worry I'm already dead. I mean, how would you really know? Do Stiffs think they're still alive? Think they're moving and talking and eating when really they're just sitting there decomposing?

I suddenly think of Roger. He's a Stiff, and the oldest one I have ever heard of. He still works in the office, though he's shut up in a back room with twenty air fresheners decorating his door. He retained his motor skills far past decomposition. In fact, he's mostly skeleton now; someone removed some of his excess skin to make it more even. Now only his hands remain and he uses them to continue typing numbers over and over again. There has to be a joke in there somewhere about death and taxes but Lisa was the funny one, not me.

Does Roger think he is still alive, clocking in his hours and going home to his wife every night and not a government-funded At Rest Home for Post Mortem Employees? I wonder how things look from his perspective.

He's dead, I have to remind myself. Things don't look like anything from his perspective. His eyes are gone. His brain is a pile of mush. He doesn't have thoughts or dreams. I'm really losing it today.

At 5pm on the dot I stand up from my desk and look around, my neck popping as I do. No one else moves, too absorbed in their work to realize the day is over. Even as I pack my things I wonder why I'm rushing to be the first one out. It's not like I have anything to return home to.

A seventeen-minute walk later, I'm back at an empty apartment that is exactly the way I left it this morning. Nothing's been moved or cleaned. Nothing has even been added to the slight mess. That's one of the weird things about finding yourself suddenly living alone. I could leave the kitchen counter clean and it would stay that way for days. No paprika spilled and caught in the crevices of the tile, no half-washed pan with the remnants of a failed cooking experiment in the sink. Not even an empty coffee cup on the table or a pair of shorts left on the bedroom floor.

I change out of my suit and think about going to the gym, but end up sitting on the couch and watching some sitcom about a guy and his Stiff twin brother playing pranks on people. There's something comedic about watching actors portray Stiffs on TV. Their chests still move up and down with breath and despite the contact lenses, you can still see a light in their eyes.

I don't know how long I've been sitting there watching episodes roll right into another, when the phone suddenly rings. I reach for it, dreading seeing the lawyer's number on it again, but instead the caller ID is long and strange. I cautiously pick up.

"Hello?"

"Hi, is this Mr. Keller?"

"Uh, yes, may I ask who's calling?"

"This is Antony Ward from San Fran General. We have a female Post Mortem here whose family we've been trying to track down for a while. It appears she might belong to you."

My first thought is Lisa and my entire body goes ice cold.

"What...what was her name?"

He doesn't seem to hear my whisper and keeps talking.

"...a trolley and three cars, lots of Sti-I mean Post Mortems just standing around, we don't have anywhere to put them. They're getting in the way of the living patients. We know it's a delicate situation, but we really need family members to come as soon as possible to claim them. When can you be here?"

It takes me a full thirty seconds to respond.

"I'm on my way."

I take the bus to the hospital because I can't remember where Lisa last parked the car. It hits me that she might never drive again. The whole way there my mind spins in twenty different directions and every train of thought ends in despair. I resort to numbers, hoping their simplicity will keep me sane. If the bus stops for twenty seconds at each stop and the hospital is seven stops away I'll arrive right at 10:13.

I am only off by thirty-six seconds, according to my watch, because I underestimated the speed to which dread would propel me. When I arrive at the hospital and walk in the front doors I'm greeted by a dozen Stiffs, some standing, some sitting, but all staring as if they have been assigned different points on the wall to study meticulously. All bear the signs of the gruesome collision. Bloodied clothes, a few missing limbs, gashes. The living patients in the waiting room huddle in a corner opposite them, nursing their various afflictions and trying not to look at the Stiffs. Trying not to think about how they might join their ranks if their injuries aren't treated soon.

With difficulty, I make my way to the front desk and give the frazzled nurse my name.

"Collecting a Stiff? Post Mortem, I mean. Sorry, still getting used to the politically correct. Name?"

"James Keller."

"No, the name of the deceased?"

"Oh, um…"

"It's all right I have it here. Keller. She's this way, follow me."

I swallow and let the nurse lead me to a back corner. Each step weighs a million pounds. She positions me in front of a slender Stiff woman with black hair and numerous tattoos lining her arms, which are grazed with shallow gashes. Her clothes have been mostly ripped away in the accident, and now she wears tiny black shorts and half a shirt, with torn stockings down her legs. Her shoes have been lost apparently, but she still has a pink band-aid wrapped around her big toe, which pokes out of a hole in the tights. The outfit was once black, but has faded to a dull brown color, stiffened by blood. She's dead, but you can still see she's gorgeous. She wears bright red lipstick, and dark eye shadow rims her eyes, which have glossed over and do not see. A short, round, metal pipe protrudes from the side of her skull.

It is most decidedly not Lisa.

"I'm afraid there's been some mistake," I say with difficulty. The sense of relief is so strong, I can hardly speak.

"Right, the pipe, sorry about that. Doctor said removing it would cause the entire cranium to collapse and he wanted to leave it up to the family member."

"But I'm not…"

"It took us forever to find a contact. These types of women, they don't…well, they don't typically give their real name in their profession, if you know what I mean."

She looks incredibly embarrassed and I realize that the woman's outfit was in fact not destroyed in the accident.

"But she's been in before for…uh…medical testing, so we finally found the name Amelia Keller. She put you down as an emergency contact."

"She did?" I study her again, but no recognition comes to me.

The nurse's face softens. "I'm so sorry for your loss sir. I have to go attend to other patients now, just fill out these forms and custody of the deceased passes to you."

She hands me a clipboard and pen and bustles away, carefully nudging a Stiff in a shredded business suit back into place against the wall as she goes.

I turn back to the dead girl and examine her. I'm fairly sure there is no one named Amelia in my family. Certainly no hookers named Amelia in the family. So is this merely a coincidence? Was there another James Keller, or was that simply a random name she exchanged on paperwork for medical treatment?

She stands next to me and offers no answers. She seems to be patiently waiting for me to decide whether or not I want her. It strikes me as the saddest thing I've ever seen. Like a puppy at the pound trying not to get its hopes up when you walk in the door. Trying to look indifferent if you leave.

Before I know what I'm doing, I sign my name at the bottom of the clipboard and deposit it back at the front desk. I can't say for sure why, but I have a feeling if I don't claim her, no one will. I take the Stiff by the hand, and lead her out of the building.

As I put one foot in front of the other, I'm surprised by how calm and confident my steps are. It's as if my body knows what it's doing while my mind panics.

I have no idea what to do with her. Put her in an At Rest Home? How much do those places cost? A Stiff Homeless Shelter? I could just dump her somewhere on the street, let someone else take care of her.

I pause at the bus stop. When I stop, she stops and I think how odd it is, the way she follows me. Like a shadow. How do you just dump someone like that? Someone who can't help but trust and follow.

*What are you thinking James? She can't trust. She's dead!*

When the bus pulls up, my legs automatically step up two stairs and I dig around for some extra change. I'm not sure where we're going yet, but it's an action I feel I can trust.

"No Stiffs allowed," a gruff voice says.

I look up surprised at the bus driver. "What do you mean?"

"No Stiffs. They stink up the place. Decompose all over the seats. Can't tell you the number of times people have just left a Stiff on the bus. Driven them around all night and had to take them to a Shelter. Too much hassle. No Stiffs."

I glance back at the girl, wondering if I should just leave her on the bench, get on the bus and go home. The way she stares at the street it's almost as if she knows what I'm thinking. Knows she's powerless to persuade me one way or the other. All she can do is stare and wait for my decision.

Again I'm struck by the fact that this woman's life (or death) is in my hands. It's a responsibility I've never had before. It's unnerving, and as irrational as it is, I feel like I can't let her down. I know I'm being ridiculous. She doesn't care one way or the other. I have no ties to this Stiff. But I signed for her, like some strange package. In that action I assumed at least partial responsibility. If I just leave her, who knows what kind of person will find her? She might sit here for weeks before someone moves her. I can at least get her somewhere safe before I take off.

I step off the bus, still uncertain but at least partially decided. The driver shrugs and closes the doors in my face. As the bus speeds away, I peek a glance at the Stiff's face to see any sign of relief or thanks, but it is carefully indifferent, watching the streetlamp. Stiffs always seem to be attracted to light. I never understood why.

"Let's go."

The Stiff doesn't reply.

I start walking in the general direction of my apartment, and again the Stiff walks with me. I'm hoping that somewhere in the next forty blocks an idea or burst of inspiration will hit.

Everything I walk by becomes an option for a way out. I pass bars already crowded with drunks. I could leave her in there. Surely the bartenders have dealt with a few Stiffs left behind before. But I keep walking.

I pass a park, mainly occupied by the homeless. I could leave her on the bench, like the Stiff listening to poetry. But a sudden image of a child discovering the Stiff during his morning play horrifies me.

In a seedier part of town, I pass a Stiff brothel. A man in a black jacket slinks out with a sweaty forehead. There are laws against necrophilia, but it's hard to enforce rights on dead people who don't even know what's going on around them. I could drop the girl there. It's not like she would care, and judging from her outfit and the nurse's implications, she would probably feel right at home. But even as I think it I know I'll walk right past the joint. Disgusted with myself.

I feel the strangest urge to call Lisa. For some reason I just know she would know exactly what to do. But I don't make a move to pull out my cell phone. I don't make any movements except to keep walking. I am as incapable of action or decisions as the Stiff who shadows me.

Suddenly the answer appears, ironically, like a miracle. A Church! The towering spirals of St. Mary's are like a beacon of hope. Surely a church will know what to do with her! They will take care of her, find a place for her, pray for her, all that other saintly stuff. There's no way I could feel guilty about leaving her there.

I guide the Stiff up the stairs and knock on the towering wooden doors. A tired looking priest sticks his head pleasantly through the door, but when he sees the Stiff with me, his smile falters slightly.

"Another one? This city is falling apart."

"Uh, right. Can you take care of her for me?"

The priest is reluctant. "It's just...we already have so many tonight. So many people bring their deceased to us to care for, pray for, until their earthly bodies are retired, but we're a little overwhelmed. Is there anyway you could...just...keep her for the night?"

"I'm sorry?"

"You see, we have volunteers coming in the morning to help us. They take the Stiffs to safe places. They're a true blessing. But tonight it's just me and I already have six..."

Seeing the look on my face, his takes on a pitying expression. He pats my arm sympathetically. "I know it's not easy for some, to be forced to endure their loved ones in this state. Take heart, my son. Her spirit is with the Lord. This empty shell, this earthly form, is not really her. Watching it decay is difficult, I understand. But be comforted that her spirit has been freed from fleshy limitations."

"Right," I say, never really being religious myself. "And you can't take her...fleshy form tonight?"

He sighs.

"Of course, I would never turn away someone in need. The Church bids me to accept and I…"

"You know what, it's fine," I say suddenly. "I'll bring her back in the morning."

"Bless you, son. We all have our crosses to bear. But in the morning, we'll make sure your friend is well taken care of."

He seems so relieved to not have to take in another decaying body. And I can't blame him. Her unrelenting stare and putrefying flesh are started to wear on me. I can't imagine what it would be like to spend the night with multiple dead all alone in a big dark church.

So the Stiff and I end up back at my apartment. It feels rather like that time my cousin Claire asked me to babysit her one-year-old daughter. I had no idea what to do with the child, who lay in her crib and stared at the ceiling much like the Stiff is doing now. Eventually, the baby was hungry or needed changing, but the Stiff just stands still while I run around, trying to clean up the mess (though she can't see it or care), turning the AC on full blast (I read somewhere that keeping it cold helps keep the flesh preserved better), and laying dozens of blankets on the couch before I help her sit on it.

Just like with the baby, once she's settled I sit staring at her staring at the lamp in the corner. Now what?

I take a breath. What would I be doing if she weren't here? So I flick the tv on, to the marathon of the show I was watching earlier. Her eyes slowly (and if I'm being honest, a little unnervingly) travel to its bright blue glow.

"Right." I say the word slowly, testing out the noise in the silent apartment. "Well, this isn't the best show, and I know because I watched several episodes earlier, but it has some funny moments." Once I start, I can't seem to stop. "Sorry about the couch. It's uncomfortable, I know. Lisa, my ex-wife, she bought it to match the coffee table. I mean, who buys a couch to match the coffee table? It was her grandmother's coffee table, apparently. And now she's gone and taken the table and left the couch, and I'm stuck with it because I can't shell out hundreds of dollars on a new one when this one is here and functional."

The Stiff doesn't reply. I don't expect her to, which is one positive sign that I'm not going crazy. Seeing her sit there as the temperature drops in her half shirt brings out an old, almost forgotten instinct in me. I slip into the bedroom and dig through the closet until I find an old sweater Lisa left behind. I awkwardly wrap it around the Stiff's shoulders, brushing her cold skin. Strangely, I don't feel the urge to shudder away.

"Hope you don't mind that this was hers. She never came to collect the rest, and though my attorney says I'm well within my rights to trash it all, I just couldn't bring myself to. I'm not sentimental, really, I just kept it in case she ever wanted it back."

I take a seat on the armchair, awkwardly fidgeting. I try not to look at her too much.

"Oh, this one is pretty good. The living twin dresses up the Stiff twin and tries to make him take his place in a spelling bee."

I force myself to watch a few episodes of the horrid comedy show. It's incredibly uncomfortable at first, but as each new episode starts I find it easier and easier to relax. My body adjusts so quickly to having someone home again. It's surprisingly nice. It reminds me of the nights Lisa and I would just sit and watch TV. In the good days when we didn't argue. When the silence was an indication of our familiarity and not anger.

Eventually, my eyes start dropping. I stretch and yawn,

glancing at the Stiff out of the corner of my eye. She makes no movement.

"I'm heading to bed," I say, a bit louder than normal. "I'll leave the tv on. I'll take you back to the church in the morning."

I wait a second, and when she doesn't reply I cross over to my bedroom. I consider locking the door, but decide against it. She's not going anywhere. I crawl into bed and think about how it's going to take me forever to fall asleep knowing there's a strange, dead girl in my apartment. But surprisingly, I'm out within minutes and have the best night's sleep since Lisa left.

In the morning, it takes me a few moments to remember everything that's happened. To remember that there's a Stiff girl sitting on my couch watching TV. For some reason I feel more nervous, less confident in the morning light. Thank God I'm taking her to the church today. I can't imagine having her hover all day, sitting in the corner like a decorative ornament or side table. I dress quickly in my suit and tie, brush my teeth, linger in the bedroom, before opening the door to the living room.

She's moved. She is not sitting upright on the couch watching the morning news as I expected her to be. Like a moth, she's drifted to the kitchen table, to the window next to it where she's watching the blinding sun peeking over the tops of the buildings. The sudden anxiety I feel at her movement quickly gives way to something else. Something much harder to define.

I think that if she had stayed where she was, perched on the end of the couch blankly watching tv, I would have gone through with it. I would have taken her to the church, given her to the priest with the sad eyes, and that would have been the end of it. I might have called up Lisa to tell her that story. Maybe we would have shared a moment, or maybe she would think I was crazy. But it would have been over and I'd be back at my life.

But seeing her at the kitchen table, I know I won't do it. Because something changed in the night. It wasn't huge; she didn't make a mess of the kitchen or even flick off the tv. But she moved. The apartment is not exactly as I left it. Here is proof that there is someone else here. Someone dead, sure, but someone.

And so I take off my tie and pour myself a bowl of cereal. I sit down across from her at the kitchen table. She doesn't look at me, keeping her eyes on the window and the sun. But I eat my breakfast and start thinking about where I can take her for lunch.

# THE LOTTERY WINNER

## Margrét Helgadóttir

Margrét Helgadóttir is a Norwegian-Icelandic writer and editor living in Copenhagen. This is her third story published in Luna Station Quarterly. http://margrethelgadottir. wordpress.com

The man screams when I open the rocket door. They often do. Maybe it's my intimidating height, or the shining metal in my suit. But I suspect it's my eye bulbs dangling on their stalks that distresses them.

Earth's cold night air ripples soothingly over my gills. I'm still shaken from the rough landing. The craft is overdue for its yearly overhaul. Vera nags me about it—bless her six tentacles—because I keep postponing it. I have no patience for the swartiers who run the rocket garage on Jupiter, or their annoying thousands of questions and endless forms to fill out. I swear, one day I'm going to chop off their tails and send them all back to Section 3.

The man takes a step back and stares at me. Maybe this one's tougher than the others I've come across. The humans. So certain they are alone in the universe. I love it when they realize this is just an illusion. I've been to Earth regularly over the years, but this is the first time I'm here on an official assignment.

I notice that my rocket's tail has sliced off the top of the garden hedge and made quite a hole in the man's backyard.

"Sorry about the hole," I chitter, my teeth clicking. I stretch out an apologetic tentacle towards him, but stop midair when he cringes.

I straighten my back. "Greetings. I'm Ikkus Hag, representing the Southern World Alliance. I'm pleased to inform you that you are this year's lucky winner of the SWA Annual Galactic Lottery. Congratulations!"

Excited, I stretch all my tentacles in the air and wait for his response.

For years now, this has been one of my favourite assignments. The names of all the Galaxy's residents are in the lottery pot from the day they are born, so it's an astonishing bit of luck to be picked out. The eyes of the winners when they realize their fortune—I love that. The lottery prize is overwhelming: a luxury house on Mars and a holiday cabin at Vepolis, a Model 094 rocket—my favourite, but I can't afford one—a dinner with the president of the Alliance, a cruise to Saq, and enough money to have a comfortable life.

This man is the first Earthling to win the lottery and I know it will bring him fame and a neverending series of dinners and exciting invitations. And possibilities—after all, one of the early winners is now the Vice President of the Alliance.

The man is wide-eyed and silent. I'm starting to wonder if he's dumb or just shocked beyond words, when he turns around abruptly and disappears into his house. I lower my tentacles. Probably fetching his family, I figure. Must want to share the good news. I rub my tentacles against the rocket's matte surface in an effort to polish it. It's stained and there's a rift on one side. I'd better get the rocket to Jupiter after this assignment.

The man is back. He's carrying something in his arms. It glints in the moonlight. He's pointing it towards me. A gift for me? He must be so happy. I click my teeth in excitement.

He's yelling now: "Hooo mi hasi tki!"

"What?" I squeal in confusion. Why can't I understand what he says? Where's my linguistic device? Have I forgotten to turn it on? I poke my tentacles into all my pockets, but cannot find it. Have I left it at home?

If I can't understand him, he can't understand me. So he doesn't know he's won the lottery. Frustrated, I bang my tentacles on the rocket—doonk doonk—and look up.

"Ta ta hokk," the man shouts. He sounds angry.

"Yes, I'm angry too," I mutter, and glide back into my rocket, turning my eye bulbs to watch him as I move. The last thing I see before my door closes—swoosh—is him aiming his shiny thing at me and firing it. Finally, the craft stops shaking from the explosion and I study the interior. Undamaged, but Jupiter next stop for sure.

Feeling cheerfully again, I wave my tentacles at him. "I'll be back."

# THANK YOU

Many thanks to our patrons
and supporters, especially:

KE Jaeck

Tory Hoke

GriffinFire


Want to see your name here? Become a patron!
patreon.com/lunastation

 patreon

# ABOUT THE COVER ARTIST

Sara Kipin is currently a senior illustration major attending the Maryland Institute College of Art in Baltimore. As a child, she was gifted many illustrated fantasy books from her family and has now taken that inspiration with her into her adult years. Once graduated, she hopes to use these aesthetics as a book illustrator or a preproduction artist.

Learn more about Sara and see her work at:
http://sarakipin.tumblr.com

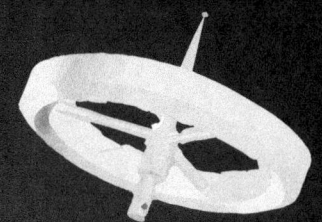

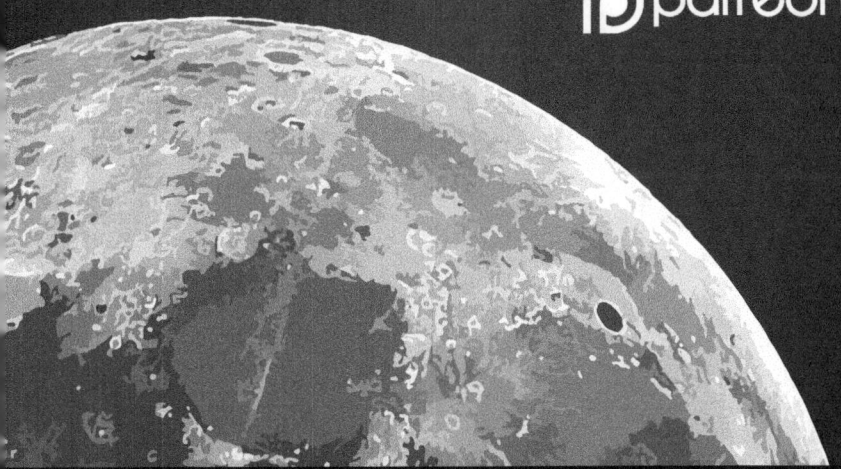

www.ingramcontent.com/pod-product-compliance
Lightning Source LLC
Chambersburg PA
CBHW060054150626
46556CB00017BA/676